DEADLY FORMULA

"Now tell me—when your transmuter is completed, what can you *do* with this thing?"

"Well"—Craig removed his goggles and brushed his hair back—"I could probably prevent any kind of projectile, or plane, from entering the earth's atmosphere over a controlled area."

"Neutralizing the potential of atomic warfare?"

"I suppose it would."

Nayland Smith snatched the goggles from his eyes. "Do you realize what this means?"

"Clearly. What?"

"*You're* the reason New York has become a hotbed of spies! This thing is a hundred times bigger than I suspected. Russia, I know, has an agent here. And I have reason to believe that our own land of hope and glory is onto you as well. London can't afford to let this thing fall into the hands of Moscow—nor can Washington. And none of 'em would like Dr. Fu Manchu to get it."

"Dr. Fu Manchu? I imagined it to be a mere name to frighten children."

"Wrong again, Craig. He is here—in New York. Good God, if ever a man played with fire without knowing it, you are that man. We've got to get that formula out of here—*now.*"

The master of evil returns in the

FU MANCHU mysteries

by Sax Rohmer

THE DRUMS OF FU MANCHU	(1617, $3.50)
THE TRAIL OF FU MANCHU	(1619, $3.50)
THE INSIDIOUS DR. FU MANCHU	(1668, $3.50)
DAUGHTER OF FU MANCHU	(1818, $3.50)
SHADOW OF FU MANCHU	(1870, $3.50)

CLASSIC MYSTERIES

by Mary Roberts Rinehart

THE HAUNTED LADY	(1685, $3.50)
THE SWIMMING POOL	(1686, $3.50)
THE CIRCULAR STAIRCASE	(1723, $3.50)
LOST ECSTASY	(1791, $3.50)
MISS PINKERTON	(1847, $3.50)

Available wherever paperbacks are sold, or order direct from the Publisher. Send cover price plus 50¢ per copy for mailing and handling to Zebra Books, Dept. 1870, 475 Park Avenue South, New York, N.Y. 10016. DO NOT SEND CASH.

THE SHADOW OF
FU MANCHU

by Sax Rohmer

ZEBRA BOOKS
KENSINGTON PUBLISHING CORP.

chapter 1

"Who's the redhead," snapped Nayland Smith, "lunching with that embassy attaché?"

"Which table?"

"Half-right. Where I'm looking."

Harkness, who had been briefed by Washington to meet the dynamic visitor, was already experiencing nerve strain. Sir Denis Nayland Smith, ex-chief of the Criminal Investigation Department of Scotland Yard, spoke in a Bren-gun manner, thought and moved so swiftly that his society, if stimulating, was exhausting.

Turning, when about to light a cigar, Harkness presently discovered the diplomat's table. The grill was fashionable for lunch, and full. But he knew the attaché by sight. He turned back again, dropping a match in a tray.

"Don't know. Never seen her before."

"Haven't you? *I* have!"

"Sorry, Sir Denis. Is she important?"

"A woman who looks like that is always important. Yes, I know her. But I haven't quite placed her."

Nayland Smith refilled his coffee cup, glanced

reluctantly at a briar pipe which appeared to have been rescued from a blast furnace, and then put it back in his pocket. He selected a cigarette.

"You don't think she's a Russian?" Harkness suggested.

"I know she isn't."

Smith surveyed the crowded, panelled room. It buzzed like an aviary. Businessmen predominated. Deals of one sort or another hung in the smoke-laden air. Nearly all these men were talking about how to make money. And nearly all the women were talking about how to spend it.

But not the graceful girl with that glowing hair. He wondered what she was talking about. Her companion appeared to be absorbed, either in what she was saying or in the way she said it.

And while Nayland Smith studied many faces, Harkness studied Nayland Smith.

He had met him only once before, and the years had silvered his hair more than ever, but done nothing to disturb its crisp virility. The lean, brown face might be a trifle more lined. It was a grim face, a face which hid a secret, until Nayland Smith smiled. His smile told the secret.

He spoke suddenly.

"Strange to reflect," he said, "that these people, wrapped up, airtight, in their own trifling affairs, like cigarettes in cellophane, are sitting on top of a smouldering volcano."

"You really think so?"

"I know it. Why has a certain power sent all its star agents to the United States? What are they trying to find out?"

6

"Secret of the atom bomb?"

"Rot! There's no secret about it. You know that as well as I do. Once a weapon of war is given publicity, it loses its usefulness. I gain nothing by having a rock in my boxing-glove if the other fellow has one too. No. It's something else."

"England seems to be pretty busy?"

"England has lost two cabinet ministers, mysteriously, in the past few months." All the time Smith's glance had been straying in the direction of a certain party, and suddenly: "Right!" he rapped. "Thought I was. Now I'm sure! This is my lucky day."

"Sure of what?" Harkness was startled.

"Man at the next table. Our diplomatic acquaintance and his charming friend are being covered."

Harkness craned around again.

"You mean the sallow man?"

"Sallow? He's Burmese! They're not *all* Communists, you know."

Harkness stared at his cigar, as if seeking to concentrate.

"You're more than several steps beyond me. No doubt your information is always ahead of mine. But, quite honestly, I don't understand."

Nayland Smith met the glance of Harkness's frank hazel eyes, and nodded sympathetically.

"My fault. I think aloud. Bad habit. There's hardly time to explain, now. Look! They're going! Have the redhead covered. Detail another man to keep the Burmese scout in sight. Report to me, here. Suite 1236."

The auburn-haired girl was walking towards the exit. She wore a plain suit and a simple hat. Her companion followed. As Harkness retired speedily, Nayland Smith dropped something which made it necessary for him to stoop when the attaché passed near his table.

Coming out onto Forty-sixth Street, Harkness exchanged a word with a man who was talking to a hotel porter. The man nodded and moved away.

Manhattan danced on. Well-fed males returned to their offices to consider further projects for making more dollars. Females headed for the glamorous shops on New York's Street-Called-Straight: Fifth Avenue, the great bazaar of the New World. Beauty specialists awaited them. Designers of Paris hats. Suave young ladies to display wondrous robes. Suave young gentlemen to seduce with glittering trinkets.

In certain capitals of the Old World, men and women looked, haggard-eyed, into empty shops and returned to empty larders.

Manhattan danced on.

Nayland Smith, watching a car move from the front of the hotel, closely followed by another, prayed that Manhattan's dance might not be a *danse macabre*.

When presently he stepped into a black sedan parked further along the street, in charge of a chauffeur who looked like a policeman (possibly because he was one), and had been driven a few blocks:

"Have we got a tail?" Smith snapped.

"Yes, sir," the driver reported. "Three cars behind us right now. Small delivery truck."

"Stop at the next drugstore. I'll check it."

When he got out and walked into the drugstore the following truck passed, and then pulled in higher up.

Nayland Smith came out again and resumed the journey. Two more blocks passed:

"Right behind us," the driver reported laconically.

Smith took up a phone installed in the sedan and gave brief directions. So that long before he had reached his destination the truck was still following the sedan, but two traffic police were following the truck. He had been no more than a few minutes in the deputy commissioner's office on Centre Street before a police sergeant came in with the wanted details.

The man had been pulled up on a technical offense and invited, firmly, to produce evidence of his identity. Smith glanced over the report.

"H'm. American citizen. Born in Athens." He looked up. "You're checking this story that he was taking the truck to be repaired?"

"Sure. Can't find anything wrong with it. Very powerful engine for such a light outfit."

"Would be," said Smith drily. "File all his contacts. He mustn't know. You have to find out who really employs him."

He spent a long time with the deputy commissioner, and gathered much useful data. He was in New York at the request of the Federal Bureau of Investigation, and had been given almost autocratic powers by Washington. When, finally, he left, he had two names pencilled in his notebook.

They were: Michael Frobisher, and Dr. Morris Craig, of the Huston Research Laboratory.

Michael Frobisher, seated in an alcove in the library of his club, was clearly ill at ease. A big-boned, fleshy man, Frobisher had a powerful physique, with a fighting jaw, heavy brows—coal-black in contrast to nearly white hair—and deep-set eyes which seemed to act independently of what Michael Frobisher happened to be doing.

There were only two other members in the library, but Frobisher's eyes, although he was apparently reading a newspaper, moved rapidly, as his glance switched from face to face in that oddly furtive manner.

Overhanging part of the room, one of the finest of its kind in the city, was a gallery giving access to more books ranged on shelves above. A club servant appeared in the gallery, moving very quietly—and Frobisher's glance shot upward like an anxious searchlight.

It was recalled to sea level by a voice.

"Hello, Frobisher! How's your wife getting along?"

Frobisher's florid face momentarily lost color. Then, looking up from where he sat in a deep, leathern armchair, he saw that a third member had come in—Dr. Pardoe.

"Hello, Pardoe!" He had himself in hand again: the deep tone was normal. "Quite startled me."

"So I saw." Pardoe gave him a professional glance, and sat on the arm of a chair near Frobisher's. "Been overdoing it a bit, haven't you?"

"Oh, I don't say that, Doctor. Certainly have been kept pretty busy. Thanks for the inquiry about Stella. She's greatly improved since she began the treatments you recommended."

"Good." Dr. Pardoe smiled—a dry smile: he was a sandy, dry man. "I'm not sure the professor isn't a

10

quack, but he seems to be successful with certain types of neuroses."

"I assure you Stella is a hundred per cent improved."

"H'm. You might try him yourself."

"What are you talking about?" Frobisher growled. "There's nothing the matter with me."

"Isn't there?" The medical man looked him over coolly. "There will be if you don't watch your diet." Pardoe was a vegetarian. "Why, your heart missed a beat when I spoke to you."

Frobisher held himself tightly in hand. His wife's physician always got on his nerves. But, all the same, he wasn't standing for any nonsense.

"Let me tell you something." His deep voice, although subdued, rumbled around the now empty library. "This isn't nerves. It's cold feet. An organization like the Huston Electric has got rivals. And rivals can get dangerous if they're worsted. Someone's tracking me around. Someone broke into Falling Waters one night last week. Went through my papers. I've seen the man. I'd know him again. I was followed right here to the club today. That isn't nerves, Doctor. And it isn't eating too much red meat!"

"Hm." Irritating habit of Pardoe's, that introductory cough. "I don't dispute the fact of the burglary—"

"Thanks a lot. And let me remind you: Stella doesn't know, and doesn't have to know."

"Oh, I see. Then the attempt is known only—"

"Is known to my butler, Stein, and to me. It's not an illusion. I'm still sane, if I did have a beefsteak at lunch!"

The physician raised his sandy brows.

"I don't doubt it, Frobisher. But had it occurred to you that your later impression of being followed — not an uncommon symptom — may derive from this single, concrete fact?"

Frobisher didn't reply, and Dr. Pardoe, who had been looking down at the carpet, now looked suddenly at Frobisher.

His gaze was fixed upward again. He was watching the gallery. He spoke in a whisper.

"Pardoe! Look where I'm looking. Is that a club member?"

Dr. Pardoe did as Frobisher requested. He saw a slight, black-clad figure in the gallery. The man had just replaced a vase on a shelf. Only the back of his head and shoulders could be seen. He moved away, his features still invisible.

"Not a member known to me, personally, Frobisher. But there are always new members, and guest members — "

But Frobisher was up, had bounded from his chair. Already, he was crossing the library.

"That's some kind of Asiatic. I saw his face!" Regardless of the rule, Silence, he shouted. "And I'm going to have a word with him!"

Dr. Pardoe shook his head, took up a medical journal which he had dropped on the chair, and made his way out.

He was already going down the steps when Michael Frobisher faced the club secretary, who had been sent for.

"May I ask," he growled, "since when Chinese have been admitted to membership?"

"You surprise me, Mr. Frobisher."

The secretary, a young-old man with a bald head and a Harvard accent, could be very patriarchal.

"Do I?"

"You do. Your complaint is before me. I have a note here. If you wish it to go before the committee, merely say the word. I can only assure you that not only have we no Asiatic members, honorary or otherwise, but no visitor such as you describe has been in the club. Furthermore, Mr. Frobisher, I am assured by the assistant librarian, who was last in the library gallery, that no one has been up there since."

Frobisher jumped to his feet.

"Get Dr. Pardoe!" he directed. "He was with me. Get Dr. Pardoe."

But Dr. Pardoe had left the club.

The research laboratory of the Huston Electric Corporation was on the thirty-sixth, and top floor of the Huston Building. Dr. Craig's office adjoined the laboratory proper, which he could enter up three steps leading to a steel door. This door was always kept locked.

Morris Craig, slight, clean-shaven, and very agile, a man in his early thirties, had discarded his coat, and worked in shirt-sleeves before a drawing desk. His dark-brown hair, which he wore rather long, was disposed to be rebellious, a forelock sometimes falling forward, so that brushing it back with his hand had become a mannerism.

He had just paused for this purpose, leaning away as if to get a long perspective of his work and at the same time fumbling for a packet of cigarettes, when the office door was thrown open and someone came

13

in behind him.

So absorbed was Craig that he paid no attention at first, until the heavy breathing of whoever had come in prompted him to turn suddenly.

"Mr. Frobisher!"

Craig, who wore glasses when drawing or reading, but not otherwise, now removed them and jumped from his stool.

"It's all right, Craig." Frobisher raised his hand in protest. "Sit down."

"But if I may say so, you look uncommon fishy."

His way of speech had a quality peculiarly English, and he had a tendency to drawl. Nothing in his manner suggested that Morris Craig was one of the most brilliant physicists Oxford University had ever turned out. He retrieved the elusive cigarettes and lighted one.

Michael Frobisher remained where he had dropped down, on a chair just inside the door. But he was regaining color. Now he pulled a cigar from the breast pocket of his tweed jacket.

"The blasted doctors tell me I eat too much and smoke too much," he remarked. His voice always reminded Craig of old port. "But I wouldn't want to live if I couldn't do as I liked."

"Practical," said Craig, "if harsh. May I inquire what has upset you?"

"Come to that in a minute," growled Frobisher. "First—what news of the big job?"

"Getting hot. I think the end's in sight."

"Fine. I want to talk to you about it." He snipped the end of his cigar. "How's the new secretary making out?"

"A-1. Knows all the answers. Miss Lewis was a sad loss, but Miss Navarre is a glad find."

"Well—she's got a Paris degree, and had two years with Professor Jennings. Suits me if she suits you."

Craig's boyishly youthful face lighted up.

"Suits me to nine points of decimals. Works like a pack-mule. She ought to get out of town this week-end."

"Bring her along up to Falling Waters. Few days of fresh air do her no harm."

"No." Craig seemed to be hesitating. He returned to his desk. "But I shouldn't quit this job until it's finished."

He resumed his glasses and studied the remarkable diagram pinned to the drawing board. He seemed to be checking certain details with a mass of symbols and figures on a large ruled sheet beside the board.

"Of course," he murmured abstractedly, "I might easily finish at any time now."

The wonder of the thing he was doing, a sort of awe that he, the humble student of nature's secrets, should have been granted power to do it, claimed his mind. Here were mighty forces, hitherto no more than suspected, which controlled the world. Here, written in the indelible ink of mathematics, lay a description of the means whereby those forces might be harnessed.

He forgot Frobisher.

And Frobisher, lighting his cigar, began to pace the office floor, often glancing at the absorbed figure. Suddenly Craig turned, removing his glasses.

"Are you bothered about the cost of these experiments, Mr. Frobisher?"

Frobisher pulled up, staring.

"Cost? To hell with the cost! That's not worrying me. I don't know a lot about the scientific side, but I know a commercial proposition when I see one." He dropped down into an armchair. "What I don't know is this." He leaned forward, his heavy brows lowered: "Why is somebody tracking me around?"

"Tracking you around?"

"That's what I said. I'm being tailed around. I was followed to my club today. Followed there. There's somebody watching my home up in Connecticut. Who is he? What does he want?"

Morris Craig stood up and leaned back against the desk.

Behind him a deep violet sky made a back-cloth for silhouettes of buildings higher than the Huston. Some of the windows were coming to life, forming a glittering regalia, like jewels laid on velvet.

Dusk was falling over Manhattan.

"Astoundin' state of affairs," Craig declared—but his smile was quite disarming. "Tell me more. Anyone you suspect?"

Frobisher shook his head. "There's plenty to suspect if news of what's going on up here has leaked out. Suppose you're dead right—and I'm backing you to be—what'll this thing mean to Huston Electric?"

"Grateful thanks of the scientific world."

"Damn the scientific world! I'm thinking of Huston's."

Morris Craig, his mind wandering in immeasurable space, his spirit climbing the ladder of the stars toward higher and more remote secrets of a mysterious universe, answered vaguely.

16

"No idea. Can't see at the moment how it could be usefully applied."

"What are you talking about?" Michael Frobisher was quite his old roaring self again. "This job has cost half of a million dollars already. Are you telling me we get nothing back? Are we all bughouse around here?"

A door across the office opened, and a man came in, a short, thick-set man, slightly bandy, who walked with a rolling gait as if on the deck of a ship in dirty weather. He wore overalls, spectacles, and an eye-shade. He came in without any ceremony and approached Craig. The forbidding figure of Michael Frobisher disturbed him not at all.

"Say—have you got a bit of string?" he inquired.

"I have not got a bit of string. I have a small piece of gum, or two one-cent stamps. Would they do?"

The intruder chewed thoughtfully. "Guess not. Miss Navarre's typewriter's jammed up in there. But I got it figured a bit of string about so long"—he illustrated—"would fix things."

"Sorry, Sam, but I am devoid of string."

Sam chewed awhile, and then turned away.

"Guess I'll have to go look some other place."

As he went out:

"Listen," Frobisher said. "What does that moron do for his wages?"

"Sam?" Craig answered, smiling. "Oh, sort of handyman. Mostly helps Regan and Shaw in the laboratory."

"Be a big help to anybody, I'd say. What I'm driving at is this: We have to be mighty careful about who gets in here. There's been a bad leak. Somebody

17

knows more than he ought to know."

Morris Craig, slowly, was getting back to that prosaic earth on which normal, flat-footed men spend their lives. It was beginning to dawn upon him that Michael Frobisher was badly frightened.

"I can't account for it. Shaw and Regan are beyond suspicion. So, I hope, am I. Miss Navarre came to us with the highest credentials. In any case, she could do little harm. But, of course, it's absurd to suspect her."

"What about the half-wit who just went out?"

"Knows nothing about the work. Apart from which, his refs are first-class, including one from the Fire Department."

"Looks like he'd been in a fire." Frobisher dropped a cone of cigar ash. "But facts are facts. Let me bring you up to date—but not a word to Mrs. F. You know how nervous she is. Some guy got into Falling Waters last Tuesday night and went through my papers with a fine-tooth comb!"

"You mean it?"

Craig's drawl had vanished. His eyes were very keen.

"I mean it. Nothing was taken—not a thing. But that's not all. I'd had more than a suspicion for quite a while someone was snooping around. So I laid for him, without saying a word to Mrs. F., and one night I saw him—"

"What did he look like?"

"Yellow."

"Indian?"

"No, sir. Some kind of Oriental. Then, only today, right in my own club, I caught another Asiatic watching me! It's a fact. Dr. Pardoe can confirm it.

18

Now—what I'm asking is this: If it's what we're doing in the laboratory there that somebody's after, why am *I* followed around, and not you?"

"The answer is a discreet silence."

"Also I'd be glad to learn who this somebody is. I could think up plenty who'd like to know. But no one of 'em would be an Asiatic."

Morris Craig brushed his hair back with his hand.

"You're getting *me* jumpy, too," he declared, although his eager, juvenile smile belied the words. "This thing wants looking into."

"It's going to be looked into," Frobisher grimly assured him. "When you come up to Falling Waters you'll see I'm standing for no more monkey tricks around there, anyway." He stood up, glancing at the big clock over Craig's desk. "I'm picking up Mrs. F. at the Ritz. Don't have to be late. Expect you and Miss Navarre, lunch on Saturday."

chapter 2

Mrs. F., as it happened, was thoroughly enjoying herself. She lay naked, face downward, on a padded couch, whilst a white-clad nurse ran an apparatus which buzzed like a giant hornet from the back of her fluffy skull right down her spine and up again. This treatment made her purr like a contented kitten. It had been preceded by a terrific mauling at the hands of another, muscular, attendant, in the course of which Mrs. F. had been all but hanged, drawn, quartered, and, finally, stood on her head.

An aromatic bath completed the treatment. Mrs. F. was wrapped in a loose fleecy garment, stretched upon a couch in a small apartment decorated with Pompeian frescoes, and given an Egyptian cigarette and a cup of orange-scented China tea.

She lay there in delicious languor, when the draperies were drawn aside and Professor Hoffmeyer, the celebrated Viennese psychiatrist who conducted the establishment, entered gravely. She turned her head and smiled up at him.

"How do you do, Professor?"

He did not reply at once, but stood there looking at

her. Even through the dark glasses he always wore, his regard never failed to make her shudder. But it was a pleasurable shudder.

Professor Hoffmeyer presented an impressive figure. His sufferings in Nazi prison camps had left indelible marks. The dark glasses protected eyes seared by merciless lights. The silk gloves which he never removed concealed hands from which the fingernails had been extracted. He stooped much, leaning upon a heavy ebony cane.

Now he advanced almost noiselessly and took Mrs. Frobisher's left wrist between a delicate thumb and forefinger, slightly inclining his head.

"It is not how do *I* do, dear lady," he said in Germanic gutturals, "but how do *you* do."

Mrs. Frobisher looked up at the massive brow bent over her, and tried, not for the first time, to puzzle out the true color of the scanty hair which crowned it. She almost decided that it was colorless; entirely neutral.

Professor Hoffmeyer stood upright, or as nearly upright as she had ever seen him stand, and nodded.

"You shall come to see me on Wednesday, at three o'clock. Not for the treatment, no, but for the consultation. If some other engagement you have, cancel it. At three o'clock on Wednesday."

He bowed slightly and went out.

Professor Hoffmeyer ruled his wealthy clientele with a rod of iron. His reputation was enormous. His fees were phenomenal.

He proceeded, now, across a luxurious central salon where other patients waited, well-preserved women, some of them apparently out of the deep-freeze. He nodded to a chosen few as he passed, and entered an office marked "Private." Closing the door, he pulled out a drawer in the businesslike desk — and a bookcase filled with advanced medical works, largely German, swung open bodily.

The professor went into the opening. As the bookcase swung back into place, the drawer in the desk closed again.

Professor Hoffmeyer would see no more patients today.

The room in which the professor found himself was a study. But its appointments were far from conventional. It contained some very valuable old lacquer and was richly carpeted. The lighting (it had no visible windows) was subdued, and the peculiar characteristic of the place was its silence.

Open bookcases were filled with volumes, some of them bound manuscripts, many of great age and all of great rarity. They were in many languages, including Greek, Chinese, and Arabic.

Beside a cushioned divan stood an inlaid stool equipped with several opium pipes in a rack, gum, lamp, and bodkins.

A long, carved table of time-blackened oak served as a desk. A high-backed chair was set behind it. A faced volume lay open on the table, as well as a closely written manuscript. There were several other books there, and a number of curious objects difficult to identify in the dim light.

The professor approached a painted screen placed before a recess and disappeared behind it. Not a sound broke the silence of the room until he returned.

He had removed the gloves and dark glasses, and

for the black coat worn by Professor Hoffmeyer had substituted a yellow house robe. The eyes which the glasses had concealed were long, narrow, and emerald-green. The uncovered hands had pointed fingernails. This gaunt, upright, Chinese ascetic was taller by inches than Professor Hoffmeyer.

And his face might have inspired a painter seeking a model for the Fallen Angel.

This not because it was so evil but because of a majestic and remorseless power which it possessed—a power which resided in the eyes. They were not the eyes of a normal man, moved by the desires, the impulses shared in some part by us all. They were the eyes of one who has shaken off those inhibitions common to humanity, who is undisturbed by either love or hate, untouched by fear, unmoved by compassion.

Few such men occur in the long history of civilization, and none who has not helped to change it.

The impassive figure crossed, with a silent, catlike step, to the long table, and became seated there.

One of the curious objects on the table sprang to life, as if touched by sudden moonlight. It was a crystal globe resting on a metal base. Dimly at first, the outlines of a face materialized in the crystal, and then grew clear. They became features of an old Chinese, white-moustached, wrinkled, benign.

"You called me, Doctor?"

The voice, though distant, was clear. A crinkled smile played over the parchment face in the crystal.

"You have all the reports?"

The second voice was harsh, at points sibilant, but charged with imperious authority. It bore no resemblance to that of Professor Hoffmeyer.

"The last is timed six-fifteen. Shall I give you a summary?"

"Proceed, Huan Tsung. I am listening."

And Huan Tsung, speaking in his quiet room above a shop in Pell Street, a room in which messages were received mysteriously, by day and by night, from all over Manhattan, closed his wise old eyes and opened the pages of an infallible memory.

This man whose ancestors had been cultured noblemen when most of ours were living in caves, spoke calmly across a system of communication as yet unheard of by Western science . . .

"Excellency will wish to know that our Burmese agent was recognized by Nayland Smith in the grillroom and followed by two F.B.I. operatives. I gave instructions that he be transferred elsewhere. He reports that he has arrived safely. His notes of the conversation at the next table are before me. They contain nothing new. Shall I relate them?"

"No. I shall interview the woman personally. Proceed."

"Nayland Smith visited the deputy commissioner and has been alone with him more than two hours. Nature of conversation unknown. The Greek covering his movements was intercepted and questioned, but had nothing to disclose. He is clumsy, and I have had him removed."

"You did well, Huan Tsung. Such bunglers breed danger."

"Mai Cha, delivering Chinese vase sent by club secretary for repair, attired herself in the black garment she carries and gained a gallery above the library where Michael Frobisher talked with a medical friend. She reports that Frobisher had had sight of our agent at Falling Waters. Therefore I have transferred this agent. Mai Cha retired, successfully, with price of repairs."

"Commend Mai Cha."

"I have done so, Excellency. She is on headquarters duty tonight. Excellency can commend her himself."

"The most recent movements of Frobisher, Nayland Smith, and Dr. Craig."

"Frobisher awaits his wife at the Ritz-Carlton. Nayland Smith is covered, but no later report has reached me. Dr. Craig is in his office."

"Frobisher has made no other contacts?"

"None, Excellency. The stream flows calmly. It is the hour for repose, when the wise man reflects."

"Wait and watch, Huan Tsung. I must think swiftly."

"Always I watch—and it is unavoidable that I wait until I am called away."

Moonlight in the crystal faded out, and with it the wrinkled features of the Mandarin Huan Tsung.

Complete silence claimed the dimly lighted room. The wearer of the yellow robe remained motionless for a long time. Then, he stood up and crossed to the divan, upon which he stretched his gaunt body. He struck a silver bell which hung in a frame beside the rack of opium pipes. The bell emitted a high, sweet note.

Whilst the voice of the bell still lingered, drowsily, on the air, draperies in a narrow, arched opening were drawn aside, and a Chinese girl came in.

She wore national costume. She was very graceful,

and her large, dark eyes resembled the eyes of a doe. She knelt and touched the carpet with her forehead.

"You have done well, Mai Cha. I am pleased with you."

The girl rose, but stood, head lowered and hands clasped, before the reclining figure. A flush crept over her dusky cheeks.

"Prepare the jade pipe. I seek inspiration."

Mai Cha began quietly to light the little lamp on the stool.

Although no report had reached old Huan Tsung, nevertheless Nayland Smith had left police headquarters.

He was fully alive to the fact that every move he had made since entering New York City had been noted, that he never stirred far without a shadow.

This did not disturb him. Nayland Smith was used to it.

But he didn't wish his trackers to find out where he was going from Centre Street—until he had got there.

He favored, in cold weather, a fur-collared topcoat of military cut, which was almost as distinctive as his briar pipe. He had a dozen or more police officers paraded for his inspection, and selected one nearly enough of his own build, clean-shaven and brown-skinned. His name was Moreno, and he was of Italian descent.

This officer was given clear instructions, and the driver who had brought Nayland Smith to headquarters received his orders, also.

When a man wearing a light rainproof and a dark-blue felt hat (property of Detective Officer Moreno) left by a side entrance, walked along to Lafayette Street, and presently picked up a taxi, no one paid any attention to him. But, in order to make quite sure, Nayland Smith gave the address, Waldorf-Astoria, got out at that hotel, walked through to the Park Avenue entrance, and proceeded to his real destination on foot.

He was satisfied that he had no shadow.

The office was empty, as Camille Navarre came out of her room and crossed to the long desk set before the windows. One end had been equipped for business purposes. There was a leather-covered chair and beside it a dictaphone. A cylinder remained on the machine, for Craig had been dictating when he was called to the laboratory. At the other end stood a draughtsman's stool and a quantity of pens, pencils, brushes, pans of colored ink, and similar paraphernalia. They lay beside a propped-up drawing board, illuminated by a tubular lamp.

Camille placed several typed letters on the desk, and then stood there studying the unfinished diagram pinned to the board.

She possessed a quiet composure which rarely deserted her. As Craig had once remarked, she was so restful about the place. Her plain suit did not unduly stress a slim figure, and her hair was swept back flatly to a knot at the nape of her neck. She wore black-rimmed glasses, and looked in every respect the perfect secretary for a scientist.

A slight sound, the click of a lock, betrayed the

fact that Craig was about to come out. Camille returned to her room.

She had just gone in when the door of the laboratory opened, and Craig walked down the three steps. A man in a white coat, holding a pair of oddly shaped goggles in his hand, stood at the top. He showed outlined against greenish light. With the opening of the door, a curious vibration had become perceptible, a thing which might be sensed, rather than heard.

"In short, Doctor," he was saying, "we can focus, but we can't control the volume."

Craig spoke over his shoulder.

"When we can do both, Regan, we'll give an audition to the pundits that will turn their wool white."

Regan, a capable-looking technician, grey-haired and having a finely shaped mathematical head, smiled as he stepped back through the doorway.

"I doubt if Mr. Frobisher will want any 'auditions,' " he said drily.

As the door was closed, the vibrant sound ceased.

Craig stood for a moment studying the illuminated diagram as Camille had done. He lighted a cigarette, and then noticed the letters on his desk. He dropped into the chair, switching up a reading lamp, and put on his glasses.

A moment later he was afoot again, as the office door burst open and a man came in rapidly — closely followed by Sam.

"Wait a minute!" Sam was upset. "Listen. Wait a minute!"

Craig dropped his glasses on the desk, stared, and

then advanced impulsively, hand outstretched.

"Nayland Smith! By all that's holy—Nayland Smith!" They exchanged grips, smiling happily. "Why, I thought you were in Ispahan, or Yucatán, or somewhere."

"Nearly right the first time. But it was Teheran. Flew from there three days ago. More urgent business here."

"Wait a minute," Sam muttered, his eye-shade thrust right to the back of his head.

Craig turned to him.

"It's all right, Sam. This is an old friend."

"Oh, is that so?"

"Yes—and I don't believe he has a bit of string."

Sam stared truculently from face to face, chewing in an ominous way, and then went out.

"Sit down, Smith. This is a great, glad surprise. But why the whirlwind business? And"—staring—"what the devil are you up to?"

Nayland Smith had walked straight across to the long windows which occupied nearly the whole of the west wall. He was examining a narrow terrace outside bordered by an ornamental parapet. He looked beyond, to where the hundred eyes of a towering building shone in the dusk. He turned.

"Anybody else got access to this floor?"

"Only the staff. Why?"

"What do you mean when you say the staff?"

"I mean the staff! Am I on the witness stand? Well, if you must know, the research staff consists of myself; Martin Shaw, my chief assistant, a Columbia graduate; John Regan, second technician, who came to me from Vickers; and Miss Navarre, my secretary.

29

She also has scientific training. Except for Sam, the handyman, and Mr. Frobisher, nobody else has access to the laboratory. Do I make myself clear to your honor?"

Nayland Smith was staring towards the steel door and tugging at the lobe of his left ear, a mannerism which denoted intense concentration, and one with which Craig was familiar.

"You don't take proper precautions," he snapped. "*I* got in without any difficulty."

Morris Craig became vaguely conscious of danger. He recalled vividly the nervous but repressed excitement of Michael Frobisher. He could not ignore the tension now exhibited by Nayland Smith.

"Why these precautions, Smith? What have we to be afraid of?"

Smith swung around on him. His eyes were hard.

"Listen, Craig—we've known one another since you were at Oxford. There's no need to mince words. I don't know what you're working on up here—but I'm going to ask you to tell me. I know something else, though. Unless I have made the biggest mistake of my life, one of the few first-class brains in the world today has got you spotted."

"But, Smith, you're telling me nothing—"

"Haven't time. I baited a little trap as I came up. I'm going down to spring it."

"Spring it?"

"Exactly. Excuse me."

Smith moved to the door.

"The elevator man will be off duty—"

"He won't. I ordered him to stand by."

Nayland Smith went out as rapidly as he had come

30

in.

Craig stood for a moment staring at the door which Smith had just closed. He had an awareness of some menace impending, creeping down upon him; a storm cloud. He scratched his chin reflectively and returned to the letters. He signed them, and pressed a button.

Camille Navarre entered quietly and came over to the desk. Craig took off his glasses and looked up— but Camille's eyes were fixed on the letters.

"Ah, Miss Navarre—here we are." He returned them to her. "And there's rather a long one, bit of a teaser, on this thing." He pointed to the dictaphone. "Mind removing same and listening in to my rambling rot?"

Camille stooped and took the cylinder off the machine.

"Your dictation is very clear, Dr. Craig."

She spoke with a faint accent, more of intonation than pronunciation. It was a low-pitched, caressing voice. Craig never tired of it.

"Sweet words of flattery. I sound to myself like a half-strangled parrot. The way you construe is simply wizard."

Camille smiled. She had beautifully moulded, rather scornful lips.

"Thank you. But it isn't difficult."

She put the cylinder in its box and turned to go.

"By the way, you have an invitation from the boss. He bids you to Falling Waters for the week-end."

Camille paused, but didn't turn. If Craig could have seen her face, its expression might have puzzled him.

"Really?" she said. "That *is* sweet of Mr. Frobisher."

"Can you come? I'm going, too, so I'll drive you out."

"That would be very kind of you. Yes, I should love to come."

She turned, now, and her smile was radiant.

"Splendid. We'll hit the trail early. No office on Saturday."

There was happiness in Craig's tone, and in his glance. Camille drooped her eyes and moved away.

"Er—" he added, "is the typewriter in commission again?"

"Yes." Camille's lip twitched. "I managed to get it right."

"With a bit of string?"

"No." She laughed softly. "With a hairpin!"

As she went out, Craig returned to his drawing board. But he found it hard to concentrate. He kept thinking about that funny little *moue* peculiar to Camille, part of her. Whenever she was going to smile, one corner of her upper lip seemed to curl slightly like a rose petal. And he wondered if her eyes were really so beautiful, or if the lenses magnified them.

The office door burst open, and Nayland Smith came in again like a hot wind from the desert. He had discarded the rainproof in which he had first appeared, and now carried a fur-collared coat.

"Missed him, Craig," he rapped. "Slipped through my fingers—the swine!"

Craig turned half around, resting one shirt-sleeved elbow on a corner of the board.

32

"Of course," he said, "if you're training for the Olympic Games, or what-have-you, let me draw your attention to the wide-open spaces of Central Park. I *work* here—or try to."

He was silenced by the look in Nayland Smith's eyes. He stood up.

"Smith!—what is it?"

"Murder!" Nayland Smith rapped out the word like a rifle shot. "I have just sent a man to his death, Craig!"

"What on earth do you mean?"

"No more than I say."

It came to Morris Craig as a revelation that something had happened to crush, if only temporarily, the indomitable spirit he knew so well. He walked over and laid a hand on his friend's shoulder.

"I'm sorry, Smith. Forgive my silly levity. What's happened?"

Nayland Smith's face looked haggard, worn, as he returned Craig's earnest stare.

"I have been shadowed, Craig, ever since I reached New York. I left police headquarters a while ago, wearing a borrowed hat and topcoat. A man slightly resembling me had orders to come to the Huston Building in the car I have been using all day, wearing my own hat, and my own topcoat."

"Well?"

"He obeyed his orders. The driver, who is above suspicion, noticed nothing whatever unusual on the way. There was no evidence to suggest that they were being followed. I had assumed that they would be—and had laid my plans accordingly. I went down to see the tracker fall into my trap—"

33

"Go on, Smith! For God's sake, what happened?"

"This!"

Nayland Smith carefully removed a small, pointed object from its wrappings and laid it on the desk. Craig was about to pick it up, when:

"Don't touch it!" came sharply. "That is, except by the feathered end. Primitive, Craig, but deadly—and silent. Get your laboratory to analyze the stuff on the tip of the dart. *Curari* is too commonplace for the man who inspired this thing."

"Smith, I'm appalled. What are you telling me?"

"It was flicked, or perhaps blown from a tube, into Moreno's face through the open window of the car. It stuck in his chin, and he pulled it out. But when the car got here, he was quite insensible, and—"

"You mean he's dead?"

"I had him rushed straight to hospital."

"They'll want this for analysis."

"There was another. The first must have missed."

Nayland Smith dropped limply into a chair, facing Craig. He pulled out his blackened briar and began to load it from an elderly pouch.

"Let's face the facts, Craig. I must make it clear to you that a mysterious Eastern epidemic is creeping West. I'm not in Manhattan for my health. I'm here to try to head it off."

He stuffed the pouch back into his pocket and lighted his pipe.

"I'm all attention, Smith. But for heaven's sake, what devil are you up against?"

"Listen. No less than six prominent members of the Soviet Government have either died suddenly or just disappeared—within the past few months."

"One of those purges? Very popular with dictators."

"A purge right enough. But not carried out by Kremlin orders. Josef Stalin is being guarded as even *he* was never guarded before."

Craig began groping behind him for the elusive packet of cigarettes.

"What's afoot, Smith? Is this anything to do with the news from London?"

"You mean the disappearance of two of the Socialist Cabinet? Undoubtedly. They have gone the same way."

"The same way?" Craig's search was rewarded. He lighted a cigarette. "*What* way?"

Nayland Smith took the fuming pipe from between his teeth, and fixed a steady look on Craig.

"Dr. Fu Manchu's way!"

"Dr. Fu Manchu! But—"

The door of Camille's room opened, and Camille came out. She held some typewritten sheets in her hand. There was much shadow at that side of the office, for only the desk lights were on, so that as the two men turned and looked towards her, it was difficult to read her expression.

But she paused at sight of them, standing quite still.

"Oh, excuse me, Dr. Craig! I thought you were alone."

"It's all right," said Craig. "Don't—er—go, Miss Navarre. This is my friend, Sir Denis Nayland Smith. My new secretary, Smith—Miss Navarre."

Nayland Smith stared for a moment, then bowed, and walked to the window.

"What is it, Miss Navarre?" Craig asked.

"It's only that last cylinder, Dr. Craig. I wanted to make sure I had it right. I will wait until you are disengaged."

But Nayland Smith was looking out into the jewelled darkness, and seeing nothing of a towering building which rose like a lighted teocalli against the skyline. He saw, instead, a panelled grillroom where an attractive red-haired girl sat at a table with a man. He saw the dark-faced spy lunching alone near by.

The girl in the grillroom had not worn her hair pinned back in that prim way, nor had she worn glasses.

Nevertheless, the girl in the grillroom and Miss Navarre were one and the same!

chapter 3

In a little shop sandwiched in between more impos-
ing Chinese establishments, a good-looking young
Oriental sat behind the narrow counter writing by the
light of a paper-shaded lamp. The place was a mere
box, and he was entirely surrounded by mysterious
sealed jars, packets of joss sticks wrapped up in
pakapu papers, bronze bowls with perforated wooden
lids, boxes of tea, boxes of snuff, bead necklaces, and
other completely discordant items of an evidently
varied stock. The shop smelled of incense.

A bell tinkled as the door was opened. A big man
came in, so big that he seemed a crowd. He looked
and was dressed like some kind of workman.

The young Oriental regarded him impassively.

"Mr. Huan Tsung?" the man asked.

"Mr. Huan Tsung not home. How many time you
come before?"

"Seven."

The young man nodded. "Give me the message."

From some pocket inside his checked jacket the
caller produced an envelope and passed it across the
counter. It was acknowledged by another nod,

dropped on a ledge, and the big messenger went out. The young Chinaman went on writing.

A minute or so later, a point of light glowed below the counter, where it would have remained invisible to a customer had one been in the shop.

The envelope was placed in a tiny cupboard and a stud was pressed. The light under the counter vanished, and the immobile shopman went on writing. He wrote with a brush, using India ink, in the beautiful, difficult idiograms of classic Chinese.

Upstairs, in a room the walls of which were decorated with panels of painted silk, old Huan Tsung sat on a divan. He resembled the traditional portrait of Confucius. From a cupboard at his elbow corresponding to that in the shop below, he took out the message, read it, and dropped message and envelope into a brazier of burning charcoal.

He replaced the mouthpiece of a long-stemmed pipe between his wrinkled lips.

On a low-set red lacquer stool beside the divan was a crystal globe, similar in appearance to that upon the long, narrow table in the study adjoining Professor Hoffmeyer's office.

Nothing occurred for some time. Huan Tsung smoked contentedly, reflection from the brazier lending a demoniac quality to his benign features.

Then the crystal globe came to life, like a minor moon emerging from a cloud. Within it materialized a gaunt, wonderful face, the brow of a philosopher, green, fanatical eyes in which slumbered the fires of an imperious will.

Below, in the shop, but inaudible in the silk-walled room above, a phone buzzed. The patient writer laid his brush aside, took up the instrument, and listened. He replaced it, scribbled a few pencilled lines, put the paper in the cupboard, and pressed the button.

Huan Tsung, with a movement of his hand, removed the message. He glanced at it—and dropped the sheet into the brazier. The face in the globe had fully materialized. Compelling eyes looked into his own. Huan Tsung spoke.

"You called me, Doctor?"

"No doubt you have later reports."

"The last one, Excellency, just to hand, is timed 7.26 P.M. Nayland Smith left Centre Street at seven twenty-three. Our agent, following, carried out the operation successfully—"

"Successfully!" A note of anger became audible in the sibilant tones. "I may misunderstand you. What method was used?"

"B.W. 63, of which I have a little left, and the feathered darts. I instructed Sha Mu, who is expert, and he succeeded at the second attempt. He passed the police car undetected and retired in safety. Nayland Smith was taken, without being removed from the car, to the Rockefeller Institute."

Huan Tsung's eyes were closed. His features wore a mask of complacency. There was a brief silence.

"Open your eyes!" Huan Tsung did so, and shrank. "They think Professor Lowe may save him. They are wrong. Your action was ill considered. Await instructions to establish contact."

"Excellency's order noted."

"Summarise any other reports."

"There are few of importance. The Emir Omar Khan died in Teheran this morning."

"That is well. Nayland Smith's visit to Teheran was wasted. Instruct Teheran."

"Excellency's order noted. There is no later report from Moscow and none from London."

Silence fell. The green eyes in the crystal mirror grew clouded, filmed over in an almost pathological way. The cloud passed. They blazed again like emeralds.

"You have destroyed that which might have been of use to us. Furthermore, you have aroused a nest of wasps. Our task was hard enough. You make it harder. A disappearance—yes. I had planned one. But this clumsy assassination—"

"I thought I had done well."

"A legitimate thought is the child of wisdom and experience. Thoughts, like children, may be bastards."

Light faded from the crystal. Old Huan Tsung smoked, considering the problem of human fallibility.

"This is stupendous!" Nayland Smith whispered.

With Morris Craig, he stood under a dome which occupied one end of the Huston laboratory. It was opaque but contained four small openings. Set in it, rather as in an observatory, was an instrument closely resembling a huge telescope, except that it appeared to be composed of some dull black metal and had no lens.

Through the four openings, Nayland Smith could see the stars.

Like Craig, he wore green-tinted goggles.

That part of the instrument where, in a real tele-scope, the eyepiece would be, rested directly over a solid table topped with a six-inch-thick sheet of a grey mineral substance. A massive portcullis of the same material enclosed the whole. It had just been raised. An acrid smell filled the air.

"Some of the Manhattan rock below us is radioactive," Craig had explained. "So, in a certain degree, are the buildings. Until I found that out, I got no results."

Complex machinery mounted on a concrete plat-form, machinery which emitted a sort of radiance and created vibrations which seemed to penetrate one's spine, had been disconnected by Regan from its powerful motors.

In a dazzling, crackling flash, Nayland Smith had seen a lump of solid steel not melt, but disperse, disintegrate, vanish!

A pinch of greyish powder alone remained.

"Keep the goggles on for a minute," said Craig. "Of course, you understand that this is merely a model plant. I might explain that the final problem, which I think I have solved, is the transmuter."

"Nice word," snapped Smith. "What does it mean?"

"Well—it's more than somewhat difficult to define. Sort of ring-a-ring of neutrons, pocket full of plu-trons. It's a method of controlling and directing the enormous power generated here."

Nayland Smith was silent for a moment. He was dazed by the thing he had seen, appalled by its implications.

"If I understand you, Craig," he said rapidly, "this

41

device enables you to tap the great belt of ultraviolet rays which, you tell me, encloses the earth's atmosphere a hundred miles above the ionosphere—whatever that is."

"Roughly speaking—yes. The term, ultraviolet, is merely one of convenience. Like marmalade for a preparation containing no oranges."

"So far, so good. Now tell me—when your transmuter is completed, what can you *do* with this thing?"

"Well"—Craig removed his goggles and brushed his hair back—"I could probably prevent any kind of projectile, or plane, from entering the earth's atmosphere over a controlled area. That is, if I could direct my power upward and outward."

"Neutralizing the potential of atomic warfare?"

"I suppose it would."

"What about directed downward and inward?" rapped Smith.

"Well"—Craig smiled modestly—"that's all I *can* do at the moment. And you have seen one result."

Nayland Smith snatched the goggles from his eyes.

"Do you realize what this means?"

"Clearly. What?"

"It means that you're a focus of interest for God knows how many trained agents. I know now why New York has become a hotbed of spies. You don't appreciate your own danger."

Morris Craig began to feel bewildered.

"Do try to be lucid, Smith. *What* danger? Why should *I* be in danger?"

Nayland Smith's expression grew almost savage.

"Was *I* in danger today? Then tell me what became

42

of Dr. Sven Helsen—inventor of the Helsen lamp?"

"That's easy. I don't know."

"And of Professor Chiozza, in his stratoplane, in which he went up to pass out of the earth's atmosphere?"

"Probably passed out of same—and stayed out."

"Not a bit of it. Dr. Fu Manchu *destroys* obstacles as we destroy flies. But he *collects* specialized brains as some men collect rare postage stamps. How do you get in and out of this place at night when the corporation offices are closed?"

"By special elevator from the thirty-second. There's a private door on the street, used by Mr. Frobisher, and a small elevator to his office on the thirty-second. Research staff have master keys. All secure?"

"From ordinary intruders. But this thing is a hundred times bigger than I even suspected. If ever a man played with fire without knowing it, you are that man. Russia, I know, has an agent here."

"Present the moujik. I yearn to greet this comrade."

"I can't. I haven't spotted him yet. But I have reason to believe our own land of hope and glory is onto you as well."

Craig, in the act of opening the laboratory door, paused. He turned slowly.

"What on earth do you mean?"

"I mean that London can't afford to let this thing fall into the hands of Moscow—nor can Washington. And none of 'em would like Dr. Fu Manchu to get it."

"Dr. Fu Manchu? I imagined it to be a mere name to frighten children. If a real person, I thought he died long ago."

43

"You were wrong, Craig. He is here—in New York! He is like the phoenix. He arises from his own ashes."

A sense of unreality, not unmixed with foreboding, touched Morris Craig. He visualized vividly the fate of the man mistaken for Nayland Smith. But when he spoke, it was with deliberate flippancy.

"Describe this cremated character, so that if I meet him I can cut him dead."

But Nayland Smith shook his head impatiently.

"I pray you never do meet him, Craig."

Camille Navarre, seated in her room, had just put a call through. She watched the closed door all the time she was speaking.

"Yes . . . Nine-nine here . . . It has been impossible to call you before. Listen, please. I may have to hang up suddenly. Sir Denis Nayland Smith is in the laboratory. What are my instructions?"

She listened awhile, anxiously watching the door.

"I understand . . . the design for the transmuter is practically completed . . . Of course . . . I know the urgency . . . But it is terribly intricate . . . No—I have quite failed to identify the agent."

For some moments she listened again, tensely.

"Sir Denis must have told Dr. Craig . . . I heard the name Fu Manchu spoken here not an hour ago . . . Yes. But this is important: I am to go to Falling Waters for the week-end. What are my instructions?"

The door opened suddenly, and Sam came lurching in. Camille's face betrayed not the slightest change of expression. But she altered her tone.

"Thanks, dear," she said lightly. "I must hang up

44

now. It was sweet of you to call me."

She replaced the receiver and smiled up at Sam.

"Happen to have a pair o' nail scissors, lady?" Sam inquired.

"Not with me, I'm afraid. What do you want them for?"

"Stubbed my toe back there, and broke the nail. See how I'm limpin'?"

"Oh, I'm so sorry." Camille's caressing voice conveyed real sympathy. "But I think there are some sharp scissors in Dr. Craig's desk. They might do."

"Sure. Let's go look."

They crossed the empty office outside, now largely claimed by shadows except where the desk lights dispersed them. Camille discovered the scissors, which Sam examined without enthusiasm but finally carried away and promised to return.

Camille lingered until the door had closed behind him, placing two newly typed letters on the desk. Then she took off her glasses and laid them beside the letters. Her ears alert for any warning sound from the laboratory, she bent over the diagram pinned to the board. She made rapid, pencilled notes, glancing down at them and back at the diagram.

She was about to add something more, when that familiar click of a lock warned her that someone was about to come out of the laboratory. Closing her notebook, she walked quickly back to her room.

Her door closed just as Nayland Smith and Craig came down the three steps.

"Does it begin to dawn on your mind, Craig, why the intelligence services of all the great powers are keenly interested in you?"

Morris Craig nodded.

"Which is bad enough," he said. "But the devil who tried to murder you today is a bigger danger than any."

"My dear Craig, *he* didn't try to murder me. If the man who did had been caught, he would never have heard of Dr. Fu Manchu."

"You mean he'd have said so?"

"I mean it would be true. Imagine a linguist who speaks any of the civilized languages, and a score of dialects, with perfect ease; an adept in many sciences; one with the brains of three men of genius. Such a master doesn't risk his neck in the hands of underlings. No. We have to deal with a detached intellect, with a personality scarcely human."

Nayland Smith fell silent—and Craig knew that he was thinking about Moreno, the man who had suffered in his place.

"Suppose, Smith," he said, "you give your problems a rest for a while and dine with me tonight?"

"I shall be glad, Craig. Let it be at my hotel. Join me there in, say, an hour from now. But let me point out it isn't *my* problem. It's yours! When you leave, get the man, Sam, to have a taxi waiting—and keep him with you. I take it he hasn't gone?"

"No. He's somewhere about. We're night birds here. But what good is Sam?"

"He's a *witness*. You're safe provided you're not alone."

"Safe from what?"

"Abduction! Being smuggled out by the mysterious subway which has swallowed up other men of use to Fu Manchu."

"Where do they go? What use can he have for them?"

"I don't know where they go," rapped Nayland Smith, "but I suspect. As for their use—the use that the ant has for the aphides. Except that Dr. Fu Manchu milks their *brains*."

Unnoticed by either, the door of Camille's room had been slowly and silently opening for some time.

"You're beginning to get me really jumpy, Smith. You don't intend to go out alone?"

Nayland Smith shook his head grimly, putting on the topcoat which had brought disaster to poor Moreno.

"I have a bodyguard waiting below—a thing I never dreamed *I'd* stoop to! But Dr. Fu Manchu doesn't want *my* brains. He wants my life!"

"For heaven's sake, be careful, Smith. The elevator man goes off at seven o'clock. I'll see you down to the street."

"Save yourself the trouble. You have work to do. I know the way. Lend me your master key. Whoever stays here on duty can do the same for you. And remember—stick by Sam until you get to my hotel."

The door of Camille's room began to close.

chapter 4

And that night Manhattan danced on, merrily.

Restaurants were crowded with diners, later to proceed to equally crowded theaters, dance halls, bars. Broadway, a fantasy invented long ago by H.G. Wells, but one he never expected to come true, roared and glittered and threw up to the skies an angry glare visible for miles — as of Rome burning.

Whilst on top of a building taller than the towers of those early seekers, the priests of Bel, a modern wizard from Merton College, Oxford, trapped and sought to tame the savage powers which hold our tiny world in thrall. His spells were mathematical formulae, his magic circle rested on steel and concrete. Absorbed in contemplation of the purely scientific facets of his task, only now did it begin to creep upon his consciousness — an evil phantom, chilling, terrifying — that under his hand lay means whereby the city of New York might be reduced to "one with Nineveh and Tyre."

"But directed downward and inward?" Nayland Smith had asked. Morris Craig realized, in this moment of cold lucidity, that directed downward and *outward*, the secret plant so lovingly and secretly assembled in the Huston laboratory might well obliterate, utterly, a great part of Manhattan.

Manhattan danced on.

Craig studied his nearly finished diagram with new doubt—almost with distaste. In the blind race for domination, many governments, including, according to Nayland Smith, that of Great Britain, watched every step of his experiments. And Dr. Fu Manchu was watching.

The Huston Electric Corporation was not to be left in undisputed possession of this new source of power.

Assuming that these unknown watchers failed to solve the secret, and that Washington didn't intervene, what did Michael Frobisher intend to do with it?

For that matter, what did he, Morris Craig, intend to do with it?

He had to admit to himself that he had never, from the moment of inspiration which had led to these results right up to this present hour, given a thought to possible applications of the monstrous force he had harnessed.

Brushing back that obstinate forelock, he dismissed these ideas which were non-productive, merely disturbing, and sat down to read two letters which Camille Navarre had left to be signed. He possessed the capacity, indispensable to success in research, of banishing any train of thought not directly concerned with the problem before him.

But, even as he picked up the typed pages, another diversion intruded.

A pair of black-rimmed glasses lay on the desk. He

knew they were Camille's, and he was surprised that she had not missed them.

He had often wondered what defect marred those beautiful eyes, and so he removed his own glasses and put hers on. Craig's sight was good, and he aided it during prolonged work merely to combat a slight astigmatism of the left eye. His lenses magnified only very slightly.

But—Camille's didn't magnify at all!

He satisfied himself that they were, in fact, nothing but plain glass, before laying them down.

Having signed the letters, he pressed a button.

Camille entered composedly and crossed to the desk.

"It was so stupid of me, Dr. Craig," she said, "but I must have left my glasses here when I brought the letters in."

Craig looked up at her. Yes, she had glorious eyes. He thought they were very deep blue, but they seemed to change in sympathy with her thoughts or emotions. Their evasive color reminded him of the Mediterranean on a day when high clouds scudded across the sky.

She met his glance for a moment and then turned aside, taking up the typed pages and the black-rimmed glasses.

"That last cylinder was rather scratchy, and there are one or two words I'm uncertain about."

But Craig continued to look at her.

"Why wear those things at all?" he inquired. "You wouldn't miss 'em."

"What do you mean, Dr. Craig?"

"Well—they're plain glass, aren't they? Why wear

50

two bits of windowpane—in such perfectly lovely optics?"

Camille hesitated. She had not been prepared for his making this discovery, and her heart was beating very fast.

"Really, I suppose it must seem strange. I know they don't magnify. But, somehow, they help me to concentrate."

"Avoid concentration," Craig advised earnestly. "I greatly prefer you when you're relaxin'. I have looked over the letter—"

"I did my best with it."

"Your best is perfection. Exactly what I said, and stickily technical." He looked up at her with frank admiration. "Your scientific equipment is A-1 wizard. Full marks for the Sorbonne."

Camille veiled her eyes. She had long lashes which Craig felt sure were an act of God and not of Elizabeth Arden.

But all she said was, "Thank you, Dr. Craig," spoken in a tone oddly constrained.

Carrying the signed letters and her glasses, she moved away. Craig turned and looked after the trim figure.

"Slip out now," he advised, "for a plate of wholesome fodder. You stick it too closely. So long as you can give me an hour from ten onward, all's well in a beautiful world."

"Perhaps I may go out—although I'm really not hungry."

She went into her room and closed the door. For a long time she sat there, the useless glasses in her hand, staring straight before her . . . He was so kind, so delicately sympathetic. He almost apologized when he had to give orders, masking them under that affected form of speech which led many people to think him light-minded, but which had never deceived Camille.

Of course, he was brilliantly clever. One day the people of the world would wake up to find a new genius come among them.

He was so clever that she found it hard to believe he had really accepted her explanation. She had done her best on the urge of the moment, but it was only postponing the evil hour. Camille had never, before that day, met Sir Denis Nayland Smith, but his reputation made discovery certain. And he would tell Morris—

Or would he?

Meanwhile, Craig was tidying up prior to going out to join Nayland Smith. He arranged pencils, bowls of ink, and like impedimenta in some sort of order. The board to which the plan was pinned he lifted from its place and carried across the office. Before a large safe he set it down, pulled out a key-ring, manipulated the dial, and unlocked the safe.

He placed the plan inside and relocked the steel door.

This done, he returned to his desk and pressed a button on the switchboard.

"Laboratory," said a tired voice. "Regan speaking."

"I'm cutting out for some dinner, Regan. Anything you want to see me about before I go?"

"Nothing, Doctor."

"Right. Back around ten."

He stood up—then remained standing, for a moment, quite still, and listening.

The sound of a short, harsh cough, more like that of a dog who has swallowed a fragment of bone than of a human being, had reached his ears.

Crossing, he opened the office door and looked out. The landing was empty.

"Sam!" he called.

Sam appeared from somewhere, chewing industriously.

"Yes, boss?"

"Did you cough?"

"Me? No, sir. Why?"

"Thought I heard someone coughing. Stand by. I want you to come along with me in a minute."

He returned, took his jacket from a hook and put it on; then draped his topcoat over his arm. He was just reaching for his hat, when he remembered something. Dropping the coat over the back of a chair, he crossed to the door of Camille's room, rapped, and opened.

She looked up in a startled way, glancing at the glasses beside her.

"Sorry—er—Miss Navarre, but may I borrow your key? Lent mine to Nayland Smith."

Camille's eyes appeared to Craig to change color, but that faint twitch of the lip which heralded a smile reassured him.

"Certainly, Dr. Craig."

She pulled a ring out of her handbag and began to detach the key which opened both elevators and the street door. Craig watched her deft white fingers, noting with approval that she did not go in for the kind of nail varnish which suggests that its wearer has been disembowelling a pig.

And as he watched, the meaning of Camille's repressed smile suddenly came to him.

"I say!" he exclaimed. "Just a minute. Pause. Give me time to reflect."

Camille looked up.

"Yes, Dr. Craig?"

"How are you going to cut out for eats, as recommended, if I pinch your key?"

"Oh, it doesn't matter a little bit."

"Doesn't matter? It matters horribly. I'm not going to leave you locked up here in the ogre's tower with no means of escape. I firmly repeat—pause. I will borrow Regan's key."

"But—"

"There are no buts. I want you to nip out for a speck of nourishment, like a good girl."

He waved his hand and was gone.

Camille sat looking towards the door for fully a minute after it had closed.

"It may be best," said Nayland Smith, "if we dine in the restaurant here. I expect calls, too."

"Must say I'll breathe more freely," Craig admitted. "I never expected to slink around New York as if crossing enemy territory. What news of Moreno?"

Smith knocked ash from his pipe with unusual care.

"Poor devil," he said softly.

"Like that, is it?"

Smith nodded. "I went there after leaving you. His

wife had been sent for. Nice kid, little more than a child. Only married six months. Maddison Lowe is probably the ace man in his province, but he's beaten this time."

"Have they identified the stuff used?"

"No. It's nothing on the order of *curari*. And there are no tetanus symptoms. He's just completely unconscious, and slowly dying. I suppose I should feel indebted to Dr. Fu Manchu. It's evidently a painless death."

"Good God, Smith! You make me shudder. What kind of man is this?"

"A genius, Craig. He is above ordinary emotions. Men and women are just pieces on the board. Any that become useless, or obstructive, he removes. It's quite logical."

"It may be. But it isn't human."

"You are not the first to doubt if Dr. Fu Manchu is human, in the generally accepted sense of the word. Certainly he has long outlived man's normal span. He claims to have mastered the secret of prolonging life."

"Do you believe it?"

"I can't doubt it. He was elderly from all accounts when I first set eyes on him, in a Burmese forest. He nearly did for me, then—using the same method—as he has done for poor Moreno, now. And that was more years ago than I care to count."

"Good heavens! How old is he?"

"God knows. Come on. Let's get some dinner. We have a lot to talk about."

As they entered the restaurant, to be greeted by a maître d'hôtel who knew Nayland Smith, Craig saw the steely eyes turning swiftly right and left. With the ease of one who has been a target for criminals all over the world, Smith was analyzing every face in the room.

"That table by the wall," he rapped, pointing.

"I am so sorry, Sir Denis. That table is reserved."

"Reserve another, and say you made a mistake."

A ten-dollar bill went far to clinch the matter. There was some running about by waiters, whispering and side glances, to which Nayland Smith paid no attention. As he and Craig sat down:

"You note," he explained tersely, "I can see the entrance from here. Adjoining table occupied. People harmless . . ."

Whilst Morris Craig attacked a honeydew melon, Smith covertly watched him, and then:

"Highly attractive girl, that secretary of yours," he jerked casually.

Craig looked up.

"Quite agree. Highly competent, too."

"Remarkable hair."

"Ah, you noticed it! Pity she hides it like that."

"Hides her eyes, too," said Smith drily.

But Craig did not reply. He had been tempted to do so, and then had changed his mind. Instead he studied a wine list which a waiter had just handed to him. As he ordered a bottle of Château Margaux, he was thinking, "Has Camille gone out? Where has she gone? Is she doing herself well?" Yes, Camille had remarkable hair, and her eyes— For some obscure reason he found himself wondering who could have coughed in the office just before he left, and wondering, too, in view of the fact that, failing Sam, it was quite unaccountable, why he had dismissed the incident so lightly.

"The devil of it is, Craig," Nayland Smith was saying, "that Fu Manchu, who has come dangerously near to upsetting the order of things more than once, is no common criminal."

"Evidently."

"He doesn't work for personal gain. He's a sort of cranky idealist. I said tonight that I prayed you might never meet him. The prayer was a sincere one. The force which Dr. Fu Manchu can project is as dangerous, in its way, as that which you have trapped in your laboratory. Five minutes in his company would convince you that you stood in the presence of a phenomenal character."

"I'm prepared to believe you. But I don't understand how such a modern Cesare Borgia can wander around New York and escape the police!"

Nayland Smith leaned across the table and fixed his steady gaze on Craig.

"Dr. Fu Manchu," he said deliberately, "will never be arrested by any ordinary policeman. In my opinion, the plant on top of the Huston Building should be smashed to smithereens." His speech became rapid, rattling. "It's scientific lunatics like you who make life perilous. Agents of three governments are watching you. I may manage the agents—but I won't make myself responsible for Dr. Fu Manchu."

Could Morris Craig have seen the face of the Chinese doctor at that moment, he might have better appreciated Nayland Smith's warning.

In his silk-lined apartment in Pell Street, old Huan

Tsung was contemplating the crystal as a Tibetan devotee contemplates the Grand Lama. Mirrored within it was that wonderful face, dominated by the blazing green eyes.

"I am served," came sibilantly in Chinese, "by fools and knaves. We, of the Seven, are pledged to save the world from destruction by imbeciles. It seems that we are children, and blind ourselves."

Huan Tsung did not speak. The cold voice continued.

"We betray our presence, our purpose, and our methods, to the common man-hunters. Had this purpose been achieved, we should have been justified. We need so short a time. Interference, now, can be fatal. But the method employed was clumsy. This victim of your blundering must not die."

"Compassion, Excellency, is an attribute of the weak."

The compelling eyes remained fixed upon him.

"Rejoice, then, that I entertain it for you. Otherwise you would have joined your revered ancestors tonight. I am moved by expediency—which is an attribute of the wise. In the death of a police officer the seed of retribution is sown. I must remain here until my work is done. If he dies, I shall be troubled. If he survives, the affair becomes less serious. In one hour from now he will be dead—unless we act. I am preparing the antidote. It is for you to find means to administer it . . . Take instant steps."

The light in the crystal faded.

As a result of this conversation, just as Craig had begun on the sweet, Nayland Smith was called to the phone.

He was not away long. But when he came back, his face wore a curious expression. In part, it was an expression of relief—in part, of something else. As he sat down:

"A miracle has been performed in Manhattan," he said.

Craig stared. "What do you mean?"

"Moreno—"

"What! Professor Lowe has won, after all?"

Nayland Smith shook his head.

"No. Professor Lowe was beaten. But some obscure practitioner, instructed by Moreno's father, insisted upon seeing the patient. As the case was desperate, and the unknown doctor—who had practised in the tropics—claimed to recognize the symptoms, he was given permission to go ahead. Moreno would have died, anyway."

"But he didn't?"

"On the contrary. He recovered consciousness shortly after the injection which this obscure doctor administered. He is already off the danger list."

"This was a brilliant bird, Smith! He doesn't deserve to be obscure."

Nayland Smith tugged reflectively at the lobe of his left ear.

"He must remain so. The physician whose name he gave is absent in Philadelphia. Officer Moreno's father was not even aware of his son's illness."

Huan Tsung had taken instant steps. But Craig laid his spoon down in bewilderment.

"Then—I mean to say—if he was an imposter—what the devil's it all about?"

"Perfectly simple. For some deep reason we can't

hope to fathom, Dr. Fu Manchu has decided that Moreno must live. I fear he has also decided that I must die. Granting equal efficiency, what are my chances?"

chapter 5

Sam was free until nine forty-five. He studied the menus displayed outside a number of restaurants suitable for one of limited resources, before making a selection. His needs were simple, it seemed, and having finished his dinner, he moved along to a bar, mounted a stool, and ordered himself a bourbon.

Seated there, in his short leather jacket, a cap with a very long peak pushed to the back of his bullet head, he surveyed the scene through his spectacles whilst lighting a cigarette.

"You're with the Huston Electric, aren't you?" said someone almost at his elbow.

Sam turned. A personable young man, of Latin appearance, had mounted the next stool and was smiling at him amiably. Sam stared.

"What about it?" he inquired.

"Oh, nothing. Just thought I'd seen you there."

"What were *you* doing there?"

"Newspaper story. I'm a reporter."

"Is that so?"

Sam eyed the reporter from head to heels, without favor.

"Sure. Laurillard's my name — Jed Laurillard. And

I'm always out for a good story."

"Well, well," said Sam.

"Push that back and have the other half. Just going to order one myself."

"That's fine. My name's Sam."

"Sam *what*?"

"Sam."

"I mean, what's your other name?"

"Jim."

"Your name is Sam Jim?"

"You got it the wrong way around. Jim Sam."

"I never heard of it before. How do you spell it?"

"S-a-m. I got an uncle the same name."

For the decimal of a second, Laurillard's jaw hardened. Then the hard line relaxed. He slapped Sam on the back and laughed, signalling the barman.

"You're wasting your time," he declared. "You ought to be in show business."

Sam grinned, but made no reply. The second bourbon went the way of the first, apparently meeting with even less obstruction.

"This new thing Huston is bringing out," Laurillard went on. "Breaking into the news next week, isn't it?"

Sam held up his empty glass and appeared to be using it as a lens through which to count the bottles in the bar.

"Is it?" he said.

"You ought to know." Laurillard signalled the barman again. "If I could get the exact date it would be worth money to me."

"Would it? How much?"

"Well"—speculatively, he watched Sam considering his third drink—"enough to make it worth, say, fifty bucks to you."

Sam looked at Laurillard over the top of his spectacles and finished his drink. He made no other reply. Laurillard caught the barman's eye and glanced aside at Sam's glass. It was refilled.

For some time after the fourth, the barman, who was busy, lost count.

"You know what I'm talking about?" Laurillard presently inquired. "This new lighting system?"

"Sure."

"Some English scientist working on it."

"Sure."

"Well, when the story breaks its going to be big. Science news is a dollar a word these days. Hurt nobody if I got it first. You're a live guy. I spotted you first time I was up there. Never miss one. It's my business—see?"

Sam emptied his glass and nodded.

"Suppose you made a few inquiries. No harm in that. I could meet you here tomorrow. Any time you say."

"What you wanna know, exac—'xac'ly?" Sam inquired.

His glance had become oblique. Laurillard signalled the barman and leaned forward confidentially.

"Get this." He lowered his voice. "I want to know when the job will be finished. That gives me a lead. It's easy enough."

A full glass was set before Sam.

"Goo' luck," he said, raising it.

"Same to you. What time tomorrow, here?"

"Same to you—mean, same time."

"Good enough. I must rush. Hard life, reporting."

Laurillard rushed. Outside, he looked in through the window and saw Sam raising his drink to his lips, sympathetically watched by the barman. What happened after that he didn't see. He was hurrying to spot where his car was parked.

He had some distance to go, but less than twenty minutes later the doorbell jangled in that Chinatown shop where a good-looking young Oriental labored tirelessly with India ink and brush. He laid his brush aside and looked up.

"Mr. Huan Tsung?" said Laurillard.

"Mr. Huan Tsung not in. You call before?"

Laurillard seemed to be consulting his memory, but, after a momentary pause, he replied.

"Yes."

"How many time?"

"Seven."

"Give me the message."

Laurillard leaned confidentially forward.

"The man from Huston Electric is taken care of. He's too drunk to go far. What's better, I've sounded him — and I think he'll play. That's why I came to see you."

"*I* think," was the cold reply, "that you are a fool." The young Oriental spoke now in perfect English. "You have exceeded your instructions. You are new to the work. You will never grow old in it."

"But —"

"I have no more to say. I will put in your report."

He scribbled a few lines in pencil, took up his brush, and went on writing.

Laurillard's jaw hardened, and he clenched his gloved hands.

"Good-by," said the industrious scribe.

Laurillard went out.

In his report concerning Sam he had stated, quite honestly, what he believed to be true. But evidently he was mistaken.

Not three minutes had elapsed before the doorbell jangled again. A man came lurching in who walked as if on a moving deck. He wore a short leather jacket and a cap with a long peak. His eyes, seen through spectacles, were challenging. He chewed as he talked, using the gum as a sort of mute.

"Say—have you got a pipe-cleaner?" he inquired.

The young Oriental, without laying his brush down, slightly raised his eyes.

"No hab."

"What's the use of a joint like this that don't carry pipe-cleaners?" Sam demanded. He looked all around, truculently. "Happen to have a bit of string?"

"No string."

Sam chewed and glared down awhile at the glossy black head bent over the writing. Then, with a parting grunt, Sam went out.

The young Chinese student scribbled another note in pencil.

Camille sat quite still in her room for so long after Craig had gone that she lost all count of time.

He had not quite shut the door, and dimly she had become aware that he was calling Regan. She heard the sound of voices when Regan came out of the laboratory; then heard the laboratory door closed.

After which, silence fell.

The work she had come here to do grew harder every day, every hour. There were times when she rebelled inwardly against the obligations which bound her. There were other times when she fought against her heart. There was no time when her mind was otherwise than in a state of tumult.

It could not go on. But where did her plain duty lie?

The silence of the place oppressed her. Often, alone here at night — as she was, sometimes — she had experienced something almost like terror. True, always Shaw or Regan would be on duty in the laboratory, but a locked iron door set them apart. This terror was not quite a physical thing. Camille was fully alive to the fact that spies watched Morris's work. But it wasn't any attempt from this quarter which dismayed her.

A deeper terror lay somewhere in the subconscious, a long way down.

Who was Dr. Fu Manchu?

She had heard that strange name spoken, for the first time, by Morris. He had been talking to Nayland Smith. Then — she had received a warning from another source.

But, transcending this shadowy menace, fearful as the unknown always must be, loomed something else — greater.

That part of Camille which was French, and therefore realist, challenged the wisdom of latter-day science, asked if greater and greater speed, more and more destructive power, were leading men to more and greater happiness. Her doubts were not new. They had come between her and the lecturers at the

Sorbonne. She had confided them to a worthy priest of her acquaintance. But he, poor man, had been unable to give her guidance in this particular spiritual problem.

If God were a reality—and Camille, whilst not a communicant, was a Christian in her bones—surely such experiments as men of science were making today must anger Him?

In what degree did they differ from those which had called down a divine wrath on the Tower of Babel?

To what new catastrophe would this so-called Science lead the world? Morris Craig's enthusiasm for research she understood. It was this same eager curiosity which had driven her through the tedium of a science training. But did he appreciate that the world might be poisoned by the fruits of his creative genius?

Often it had come to her, in lonely, reflective moments, that the wonderful, weird thing which Morris had created might be a cause of laughter in Hell . . .

What was that?

Camille thought she had heard the sound of a harsh, barking cough.

Before her cool brain had entirely assumed command, before the subconscious, troubled self could be conquered, she was out of her room and staring all around an empty office.

Of course, it was empty.

Regan, she knew, stood watch in the laboratory. The plant ran day and night, and a record was kept of the alternations (so far inexplicable) of that cosmic force which had been tapped by the genius of Morris Craig. But no sound could penetrate the laboratory.

She opened the office door and called:

"Sam!"

There was no reply. She remembered, now, hearing Morris instructing the handyman to go somewhere with him.

A great urge for human sympathy, for any kind of contact, overcame her. She glanced at the switchboard. She would call Regan. He was a cynical English northcountryman who had admired her predecessor, Miss Lewis, and who resented the newcomer. But he was better than nobody.

Then she thought of her phone call, which had been interrupted earlier in the evening. A swift recognition of what it had meant, of what it would mean to make the same call again, swept her into sudden desolation.

What was she going to do? Her plan, her design for life, had not worked out. Something had gone awry.

She must face facts. Morris Craig had crossed her path. She could not serve two masters. Which was it to be? Once again—where did her duty lie?

Listening tensely, her brain a battlefield of warring emotions, Camille turned and went back to her room. Seated at her desk, she dialled a number, and went on listening, not to a distant ring but to the silence beyond her open door. She waited anxiously, for she had come to a decision. But for a long time there was no reply.

The silent office outside was empty. So that there was no one to see a figure, a dark silhouette against the sky, against those unwatching eyes which still remained alive in one distant tower dominating the Huston Building. It was a hulking, clumsy figure, not unlike that of a great ape. It passed along the parapet outside the office windows . . .

"Yes?" Camille had got through. "Nine-nine here."

She had swung around in her chair, so that she no longer faced the open door.

"If you please."

She waited again.

Silently the door had been fully opened. The huge figure stood there. It was that of a man of formidably powerful physique. His monstrous shoulders, long arms, and large hands had something unnatural in their contours, as had his every movement, his behavior. He wore blue overalls. His swarthy features might have reminded a surgeon of a near-successful grafting operation.

"Yes," Camille said urgently. "Can I see you, tonight—at once?"

The intruder took one silent step forward. Camille saw him.

She dropped the receiver, sprang up, and retreated, her hands outstretched to fend off horror. She gasped. To scream was impossible.

"My God!" (Unknown to herself, she whispered the words in French.) "Who are you? What do you want?"

"I—want"—it was a mechanical, toneless, grating voice—"you."

chapter 6

When Morris Craig returned to his office, it remained as he had left it, illuminated only by two desk
lights. He glanced automatically at the large electric
clock on the wall above and saw that the hour was
nine-fifty-five. He took off his topcoat and hung it
up with his hat and jacket.

He was back on time.

What had Nayland Smith said?—"You're a pure
fanatic. Some lunatic like you will blow the world to
bits one of these days. You're science drunk. Even
now, you're dancing to get away . . ."

Craig stared out of the window. Many rooms in
that towering building which overtopped the Huston
were dark now, so that he thought of a London coster
dressed in "pearlies" from which most of the buttons
had been torn off. Yes, he had felt eager to get back.

Was it the call of science—of that absorbing problem which engaged his mind? Or was it, in part at
least, Camille?

If the latter, then it simply wouldn't do. In the life
of a scientist steeped in an investigation which might
well revolutionize human society there was no place

for that sort of thing. When his work was finished—well, perhaps he might indulge in the luxury of thinking about an attractive woman.

Thus, silently, Dr. Morris Craig communed with himself—quite failing to appreciate the fact that he was thinking about an attractive woman all the time.

Nayland Smith suspected this interest. Hard to deceive Smith. And, somehow (Craig couldn't pin down the impression), he felt that Smith didn't approve. Of course, recognition had come to Craig, suddenly, staggeringly, of the existence of danger he had never suspected.

He moved among shadowy menaces. Not all of them were intangible. He had seen the hand of Dr. Fu Manchu stretch out, fail in its grasp, and then bestow life upon one given up to death.

Dr. Fu Manchu . . . No, this was not the time to involve a girl in the affairs of a man marked down by Dr. Fu Manchu.

Craig glanced towards the door of Camille's room, then sat down resolutely and touched a control.

"Laboratory," came. "Regan here."

"Thought I'd let you know I'm back, Regan. How are the readings?"

"Particularly irregular, Doctor. You might like to see them?"

"I will, Regan, presently. Nothing else to report?"

"Nothing."

Craig stood up again, and crossed to the office door, which he opened.

"Sam!"

"Hello, boss?"

Sam emerged from some cubbyhole which served

71

as his headquarters. He had discarded the leather jacket and the cap with a long peak, and was resuming overalls and eye-shade.

"Is there any need for you to hang around?"

"Sure—plenty. Mr. Regan he told me to report back. There's some job in the lab needs fixing up."

"I see." Craig smiled. "You're not just sort of killing time until I go home, so that you can dog my weary footsteps?"

Sam tried an expression of injured innocence. But it didn't suit him.

"Listen, Doctor—"

"Sir Denis tipped you to keep an eye on me until I was tucked up safely in my downy cot. Did he or didn't he?"

"Well, maybe he figures there's perils in this great city—"

"You mean, he did?"

"I guess that's right."

"I thought so. Just wanted to know." Craig took out his keys and turned. "I'm going into the lab now. Come on."

Followed by Sam, he crossed and went up the three steps to the metal door. As he unlocked it, eerie greenish-grey light shone out and a faint humming sound, as of a giant hornet's nest, crept around the office. A moment later, the door closed as they went in.

The office remained silent and empty whilst the minute hand of the clock swept the dial three times. There was an attachment which sounded the hours, and its single bell note had just rung out on the stroke of ten, when Camille came in.

She stood quite still for a moment, one hand resting on the edge of the door, her slim fingers looking curiously listless. Then she came right inside and opened her handbag. Taking out the black-rimmed glasses, she stared at them as though they were unfamiliar in some way. Her glance wandered to the clock.

It would have seemed to one watching her that the clock had some special significance, some urgent message to impart; for Camille's expression changed. Almost, she might have been listening to explicit instructions. Her gaze grew alert.

She crossed to her room and went in, leaving the door half open.

Then, again, silence fell. By ones and twos, the gleaming buttons imagined by Craig disappeared from the pearly scheme which decorated a nocturne framed by long windows.

When Craig opened the laboratory door, he paused at the head of the steps.

"Be at ease, Sam. I will not stir a yard without my keeper."

He closed and locked the door, came down, and went straight across to the safe. Resolutely he avoided looking toward Camille's room to see if she had come back.

From his ring he selected the safe key, and spun the dial. Not until he took out his big drawing board, and turned, did he see Camille.

She stood right at his elbow, in shadows.

Craig was really startled.

"Good Lord, my dear!—I thought I'd seen a ghost!"

Camille's smile was vague. "Please forgive me. Didn't—you know—I was here?"

Craig laughed reassuringly.

"Forgive *me*. I shouldn't be such a jumping frog. When did you come in?"

"A few minutes ago." He saw now that she held a notebook in her hand. "There is this letter to Dr. White, at Harvard. I must have forgotten it."

Craig carried the board over to its place and fixed it up. Camille slowly followed. When he was satisfied, he suddenly grasped her shoulders and turned her around so that the reflected light from the drawing desk shone up onto her face.

"My dear—er—Miss Navarre, you have, beyond any shade of doubt, been overdoin' it. I warned you. The letter to Dr. White went off with the other mail. I distinctly recall signing same."

"Oh!" Camille looked down at her notebook.

Craig dropped his hands from her shoulders and settled himself on the stool. He drew a tray of pencils nearer.

"I quite understand," he said quietly. "Done the same thing myself, lots of times. Fact is, we're both overtired. I shan't be long on the job tonight. We have been at it very late here for weeks now. Leave me to it. I suggest you hit the hay good and early."

"But—I am sorry"—her accent grew more marked, more fascinating—"if I seem distrait—"

"Did you cut out for eats, as prescribed?"

Craig didn't look around.

"No. I—just took a walk—"

"Then take another one—straight home. Explore the ice-box, refresh the tired frame, and seek repose.

Expect you around ten in the morning. My fault, asking you to come back."

Camille sat on the studio couch in her small apartment, trying to reconstruct events of the night.

She couldn't.

It baffled her, and she was frightened.

There were incidents which were vague, and this was alarming enough. But there were whole hours which were entirely blank!

The vague incidents had occurred just before she left the Huston Building. Morris had been wonderfully sympathetic, and his kindness had made her desperately unhappy. Why had this been so? She found herself quite unable to account for it. Their entire relationship had assumed the character of an exquisite torture; but what had occurred on this particular occasion to make the torture so poignant?

What had she been doing just before that last interview?

She had only a hazy impression of writing something in a notebook, tearing the page off, and—then?

Camille stared dreamily at the telephone standing on her bureau. Had she made a call since her return? She moved over and took up the waste-basket. There were tiny fragments of ruled paper there. Evidently she had torn something up, with great care.

Her heart beginning to beat more swiftly, she stooped and examined the scraps of paper, no larger than confetti disks. Traces of writing appeared, but some short phrase, whatever it was, had been torn apart accurately, retorn, and so made utterly undecipherable.

Camille dropped down again on the divan and sat there staring straight before her with unseeing eyes.

Could it be that she had overtaxed her brain—that this was the beginning of a nervous collapse? For, apart from her inability to recall exactly what she had done before leaving the office, she had no recollection whatever, vague or otherwise, of the two hours preceding her last interview with Morris!

Her memory was sharp, clear-cut, up to the moment she had lifted the phone on her own desk to make a certain call. This had been sometime before eight. Whether she ever made that call, or not, she had no idea. Her memory held no record of the interval between then and Morris telling her she seemed tired and insisting that she go home.

But over two hours had elapsed—two lost hours!

Sleep was going to be difficult. She had an urge for coffee, but knew that it was the wrong thing in the circumstances. She went into the kitchenette and cut herself two sandwiches. She ate them standing there while she warmed some milk. This, and a little fruit, made up her supper.

When she had prepared the bed, and undressed, she still felt wide-awake but had no inclination to read. Switching the lights off, she stood at the window looking down into the street. A number of darkened cars were parked on both sides and while she stood there several taxis passed. There were few pedestrians.

All these things she noted in a subconscious way. They had no particular interest for her. She was trying all the time to recapture those lost hours. Never in her life before had such a thing happened to her. It was appalling . . .

At last, something taking place in the street below dragged her wandering mind back to the present, the actual.

A big man — abnormally big — stood almost opposite. He appeared to be looking up at her window. Something in his appearance, his hulking, apelike pose, struck a chord of memory, sharp, terrifying, but shapeless, unresolved.

Camille watched him. His presence might have nothing to do with her. He could be looking at some other window. But she felt sure he was looking at hers.

When, as she watched, he moved away, loose-armed and shambling, she stepped to the end of the bay and followed his ungainly figure with her eyes. From here, she could just see Central Park, and at the corner the man paused — seemed to be looking back.

Camille stole across her darkened room to the lobby, and bolted and chained the door.

A wave of unaccountable terror had swept over her. Why?

She had never, to her knowledge, seen the man before. He was a dangerous-looking type, but her scanty possessions were unlikely to interest a housebreaker. Nevertheless, she dreaded the dark hours ahead and knew that hope of sleep had become even more remote.

Lowering the venetian blinds, she switched up her bedside lamp and toyed with a phial of sleeping tablets. She had known many restless nights of late, but dreaded becoming a drug addict. Finally, shrugging her shoulders, she swallowed one, got into bed, and sipped the rest of the warm milk.

She did not recall turning the light out. But, just as she was dozing off, a sound of heavy, but curiously furtive, footsteps on the stair aroused her. There was no elevator.

The sound died away—if she had really heard and not imagined it.

Sleep crept upon her unnoticed . . .

She dreamed that she stood in a dimly lighted, thickly carpeted room. It was peculiarly silent, and there was a sickly-sweet smell in the air, a smell which she seemed to recognize yet couldn't identify. She was conscious of one impulse only. To escape from this silent room.

But a man wearing a yellow robe sat behind a long, narrow table watching her. And the regard of his glittering green eyes held her as if chained to the spot upon which she stood. He seemed to be draining her of all vitality, all power of resistance. She thought of the shell of a fly upon which a spider has feasted.

She knew in her dream, but couldn't remember a word that had passed, that this state of inertia was due to a pitiless cross-examination to which she had been subjected.

The examination was over, and now she was repeating orders already given. She knew herself powerless to disobey them.

"On the stroke of ten. Repeat the time."

"On the stroke of ten."

"Repeat what you have to write."

"The safe combination used by Dr. Craig."

"When are you to await a call in your apartment?"

"At eleven o'clock."

"Who will call you?"

"*You* will call me . . ."

She was exhausted, at the end of endurance. The dim, oriental room swam around her. The green eyes grew larger—dominated that yellow, passionless face—merged—became a still sea in which she was drowning.

Camille heard herself shriek as she fought her way back to consciousness. She sprang up, choked with the horror of her dreams; then:

"Did it really happen?" she moaned. "Oh, God! What did I do last night?"

Grey light was just beginning to outline the slats of the venetian blinds.

Manhattan was waking to a new day.

chapter 7

Nayland Smith crossed and threw his door open as the bell buzzed.

"Come in, Harkness."

There was an irritable note in his voice. This was his third day in New York, and he had made no progress worthy of record. Yet every hour counted.

They shook hands. Raymond Harkness was a highly improbable F.B.I. operative but a highly efficient one. His large hazel eyes were ingenuous, almost childish, in expression, and he had a gentle voice which he rarely raised. Of less than medium height, as he stood there peeling a glove off delicate-looking fingers he might have been guessed a physician, or even a surgeon, but never a detective.

"Any news?" rapped Smith, dropping restlessly into an armchair and pointing to its twin.

"Yes." Harkness sat down, first placing his topcoat and hat neatly on a divan. "I think there is."

"Good. Let's have it."

Smith pushed a box of cigarettes across the table and began to charge his foul briar.

"Well"—Harkness lighted a cigarette—"Mrs. Frobisher had an appointment at three o'clock this afternoon with Professor Hoffmeyer, the Viennese psychiatrist who runs a business on the top floor of the Woolton Building."

"How did you know?"

"I'm having Falling Waters carefully covered. I want to find out who was responsible for the burglary there last week. Stein, the chauffeur-butler, drove Mrs. Frobisher into town, in their big Cadillac. When she had gone in, Stein's behaviour was just a bit curious."

"What did he do?"

"He parked the car, left his uniform cap inside, put on a light topcoat and soft hat, and walked around to a bar on East Forty-eighth."

"What's curious about that?"

"Maybe not a lot. But when he got to the bar, he met another man who was evidently waiting for him. One of our boys who has ears like a desert rat was soon on a nearby stool."

"Hear anything?"

"Plenty. But it wasn't in English."

"Oh!" Nayland Smith lighted his pipe. "What was the lingo?"

"My man was counted out. He reports he doesn't know."

"Useful!"

"No, it isn't, Sir Denis. But Scarron—that's his name—had a bright thought when the party broke up. He didn't tail Stein. Knew he was going back to his car. He tailed Number Two."

"Good work. Where did the bird settle?"

And when Harkness, very quietly, told him, Nayland Smith suddenly stood up.

"Got something there, Harkness," he rapped. "The job at Falling Waters may have been Soviet-inspired, and not, as I supposed, a reconnaissance by Dr. Fu Manchu. What's Stein's background?"

"Man at work, right now, on it."

"Good. What about details of the bogus doctor who saved Moreno's life? To hand, yet?"

"Yes." Harkness took out a notebook and unhurriedly turned the pages. "It's a composite picture built up on the testimony of several witnesses. Here we are." He laid his cigarette carefully on the edge of an ash-tray. "Tall; well-built. Pale, clear-cut features. Slight black moustache, heavy brows; dark, piercing eyes."

"H'm," Smith muttered. "Typical villain of melodrama. Did he carry a riding whip?"

"Not reported!" Harkness smiled, returning the notebook to his pocket. "But there's one other item. Not so definite — but something I wish you could look into personally. It's in your special province."

Nayland Smith, who had worn tracks in more carpets than any man in England, was pacing the room, now, followed by a wraith of tobacco smoke.

"Go ahead."

Harkness dusted ash into a tray and leaned back in his chair.

"For sometime before your arrival," he said, "but acting on your advice that Dr. Fu Manchu was probably in New York, we have been checking up on possible contacts in the Asiatic quarter."

"Maybe none. Fu Manchu's organization isn't primarily Chinese, or even Oriental. He's head of a group known as the Council of Seven. They have affiliations in every walk of society and in every country, as I believe. The Communists aren't the only plotters with far-flung cells."

"That may be so," Harkness went on patiently, "but as a matter of routine I had the possibility looked into. Broadly, we drew blank. But there's one old gentleman, highly respected in the Chinatown area, who seems to be a bit of a mystery."

"What's his name?"

"Huan Tsung."

"What does he look like?"

"He is tall, I am told, for a Chinese, but old and frail. I've never seen him personally."

"What!" Nayland Smith pulled up and stared. "Don't follow. Myth?"

"Oh, he exists. But he's hard to get at. Some sort of invalid, I believe. Easy enough to see him officially, but I don't want to do that. He has tremendous influence of some kind amongst the Asiatic population."

Nayland Smith tugged at the lobe of his ear reflectively.

"This aged, invisible character intrigues me," he said. "How long has he lived in New York?"

"According to police records, for many years."

"But his remarkable habits suggest that he might be absent for a long time without his absence being noticed?"

"That's true," Harkness admitted.

"For instance, you are really sure he's there now?"

"Practically certain. I have learned in the last few days, since I came up from Washington to meet you, that he has been seen going for a late drive — around eleven at night — in an old Ford which is kept in a shed not far from his shop."

"Where does he go?"

"I have no information. I have ordered an inquiry on that point. You see" — he spoke with added earnestness — "I have it on reliable grounds that Huan Tsung is in the game against us. I don't know where he stands. But —"

"You want me to try to look him over?" Nayland Smith broke in. "I might recognize this hermit! I agree with you."

He began to walk about again in his restless way. His pipe had gone out, but he didn't appear to notice it.

"I could make the necessary arrangements, Sir Denis. You might try tonight, if you have no other plans."

"I have other plans. At any hour, at any moment, Craig may complete his hell machine. In that hour, the enemy will strike — and I don't know where to look for the blow, how to cover up against it. Tell me" — Smith shot a swift glance at Harkness — "does Huan Tsung ever drive out at night *more than once?*"

Harkness frowned thoughtfully. "I should have to check on that. But may I suggest that, tonight —"

"No. Leave it to me. I'm tired of going around like an escorted tourist. I want my hands free. Leave it to me."

When Nayland Smith left police headquarters that night and set out to pick up Harkness, he might have been anything from a ship's carpenter to a bosun's mate ashore. His demands on the Bureau's fancy wardrobe had been simple, and no item of his make-up could fairly be described as a disguise.

Upon this, a sea-going walk, dirty hands, and a weird, nasal accent which was one of his many accomplishments, Nayland Smith relied, as he had relied on former occasions.

He had started early, for he had it in mind to prospect the shop of Huan Tsung before joining Harkness at the agreed spot—a point from which that establishment could conveniently be kept in view.

Whilst still some distance from Chinatown proper, he found himself wondering if these streets were always so empty at this comparatively early hour. He saw parked vehicles, and some traffic, but few pedestrians.

The lights of the restaurant quarter were visible ahead, when this quietude was violently disturbed.

A woman screamed—the scream of deadly terror.

As if this had been a reveille, figures, hitherto unseen, began to materialize out of nowhere, and all of them running in the same direction. Nayland Smith ran, too.

A group of perhaps a dozen people, of various colors, surrounded a woman hysterically explaining that she had been knocked down and her handbag snatched by a man who sprang upon her from behind.

As Smith reached the outskirts of the group, pressing forward to get a glimpse of the woman's face, someone clapped a hand on his back and seemed to be trying to muscle past. His behaviour was so violent that Smith turned savagely—at which moment he felt an acute stab in his neck as if a pin had been thrust in.

"Damn you!" he snapped. "What in hell are you up to?"

These words were the last he spoke.

Strong fingers were clasped over his mouth, a sinewy arm jerked his head back — and the stinging in his neck continued!

Nayland Smith believed (he was not in a condition to observe accurately) that the assaulted woman was giving particulars to a patrolman, that the group of onlookers was dispersing.

Making a sudden effort, he bent, twisted, and threw off his attacker.

Turning, fists clenched, he faced a tall man dimly seen in the darkness, for the scuffle had taken place at a badly lighted point. He registered a medium right on this man's chin and was about to follow it up when the man closed with him. He made no attempt to use his fists, he just threw himself upon Smith and twined powerful arms around his body, at the same time crying out:

"Officer! Come and lend me a hand!"

This colossal impudence had a curious effect.

It changed Nayland Smith's anger to something which he could only have described as cold hatred. By heavens! he would have a reckoning with this suave ruffian!

But he ceased to struggle.

Those onlookers who still remained, promptly deserted the robbed woman and surrounded this new center of interest. The officer, slipping his notebook into a tunic pocket, stepped forward, a big fellow marked by the traditional *sangfroid* of a New York policeman.

He shone a light onto the face of the tall man, who still had his arms around Nayland Smith, and Smith studied this face attentively.

He saw pale, clear-cut features, a shadowy moustache, heavy brows, and dark, penetrating eyes. The man wore a black overcoat, a white muffler, and a soft black hat. Smith noted with pleasure a thin trickle of blood on his heavy chin.

Then the light was turned upon himself, and:

"What goes on?" the patrolman asked.

"My patient grew fractious. Excitement has this effect. I think he's cooling down, though. Do you think you could lend me a hand as far as my car? I am Dr. Malcolm—Central Park South."

"Poor guy. Do what I can, Doctor."

But Nayland Smith smiled grimly. It was *his* turn.

"Listen, Officer," he said—or, more exactly, he framed his lips to say . . . for no sound issued from his mouth!

He tried again—and produced only a sort of horrible, gurgling laughter.

Then he understood.

He knew that he was in the hands of that same bogus physician who had visited Moreno—that the man was a servant of Dr. Fu Manchu.

And he knew that the stinging sensation had been caused by the point of a hypodermic syringe.

He was striken *dumb* . . .

The only sound he could utter was that imbecile laugh!

"Poor guy," muttered the officer again.

"War veteran," Dr. Malcolm explained in a low voice. The onlookers murmured their sympathy. "Japanese prison camp. Escaped from my clinic yesterday. But we shall get him right — in time — with care."

During this astounding statement, Dr. Malcolm, overconfident, perhaps, in the presence of the burly patrolman, made the mistake of slightly relaxing his hold.

The temptation was too strong for Nayland Smith. Tensing every relevant muscle in his body, he broke free. He had no foot room to haul off for a straight one, no time to manoeuvre, but he managed to register a really superior uppercut on the point of Dr. Malcolm's prominent jaw. Dr. Malcolm tottered — and fell.

Then, turning, Smith ran for his life . . . He knew nothing less was at stake.

A whistle was blown. A girl screamed. Someone shouted, "Escaped madman! Stop him!" Runners were hot on his heels.

The hunt was up!

No nightmare of the past, in his long battle with Fu Manchu, approached in its terrors those which now hounded him on. Capture meant death — and what a death! For he could not doubt that Dr. Fu Manchu intended, first, to interrogate him.

And escape?

Escape meant the life of a dumb man . . .

He saw now, plainly enough, that he had held the game in his hands if only he had kept his poise. Many things that he might have done appeared to mock him.

And throughout this time, all about him, hunters multiplied. Voices cried, "Escaped madman—stop him!" Police whistles skirled; the night became a charivari of racing footsteps.

All New York pursued him.

He tried to think as he ran.

Instinctively he had turned back the way he had come. He had a faint hope that, contrary to his orders, a detective might have been assigned to follow him. How he regretted those orders! What madness to underestimate the profound cunning of Dr. Fu Manchu . . .

Suddenly someone stepped out upon him and tried a tackle. He missed. Smith tripped the tackler (he admired his pluck) and ran on.

"Escaped madman! Stop him!"

Those cries seemed to come from all around. Once he tried to shout also, wildly anxious to test again his power of speech. Only a guttural laugh rewarded him. After that he ran in silence, wondering how long he could hope to last at that pace.

Some swift runner was hot on his heels, having outdistanced all others. But Nayland Smith had recognized a warehouse just ahead, the yard gate open, which he had passed a few minutes earlier. If he could reach it first, he still had a chance. Desperation had prompted a plan.

Then, as he raced up to the gate, something happened which was not in the plan . . . A pair of stocky figures sprang out, one on either hand!

They had been posted to intercept him—the game was up!

The man on the left Smith accounted for—and he

used his feet as well as his fists. The other threw him. He was a trained wrestler and gave not one opening. Then the pack came up. It was led by the big policeman who had muttered, "Poor guy." His were the footsteps which Smith had heard so close behind.

As he lay, face downward, in a stranglehold, this officer took charge, speaking breathlessly.

"Good work! Don't hurt him. The doctor's coming." Dimly Nayland Smith became aware of an increasing crowd. "Hand him over to me. I can manage him."

He was lifted upright and seized skillfully by the patrolman. The two thickset thugs vanished into darkness outside a ring of light cast by several flashlamps. Smith retained sufficient sanity to observe that one of them limped badly. He thought and hoped that his kick had put cancelled to his kneecap.

He opened his mouth to speak, remembered, and remained silent.

"Take it easy, brother," said the big officer sympathetically. He was still breathing hard from his run. "You're not in Japan now. I don't like holding you, but you surely can use 'em, and I'm not looking for a K.O." He steered Smith into the warehouse yard — that very haven he had prayed to reach! "We'll wait here. Hi! you!" — to the audience — "shift!"

A car came along. It pulled up opposite the gateway in which they were standing . . . and Dr. Malcolm got out! A second patrolman was with him. Dr. Malcolm's voice sounded pleasantly shaky.

"Congratulations, Officer. I shall commend you for this."

"All in the day's work," replied the man who held

Smith. "Glad to see you've snapped out of it. A nifty one, that was. Shall I get the wagon?"

"No, no." Dr. Malcolm stepped forward. "It would only excite him. Here is my chauffeur. He is used to — such cases. We can manage quite well between us. Just call me in about twenty minutes. Dr. Scott Malcolm, Circle 7-0300."

Whilst this conversation proceeded, Nayland Smith made up his mind to play the last card he held — the one he had planned to play if he could have gained temporary shelter. One arm being semi-free, although the other was pinioned behind him, he managed to pull his wallet out and to force it under the fingers of the man who held him.

That efficient officer grasped it, but did not relax his hold.

"Okay," he said in a low voice, like that of one soothing a child. "I've got it. Safe enough with me. Come along."

Smith was led to the car by Dr. Malcolm and a low-browed, grey-uniformed chauffeur, who had the face and the physique of a gorilla. Dr. Malcolm took the wheel; the chauffeur got in beside Smith.

And, as the car moved away and excited voices faded, Smith's brain seemed to become a phonograph which remorselessly repeated the words:

"Dr. Scott Malcolm . . . Circle Seven — 0-3-0-0 . . . Dr. Scott Malcolm . . . Circle Seven . . . 0-3-0-0 . . .

"Dr. Scott Malcolm . . . Circle Seven —"

chapter 8

It was on the following morning that Morris Craig arrived ahead of time to find Camille already there. He was just stripping his jacket off when he saw her at the door of her room.

"Hullo!" he called. "Why the wild enthusiasm for toil?"

She was immaculate as always, but he thought she looked pale. She did not wear her glasses.

"I couldn't sleep, Dr. Craig. When daylight broke at last I was glad to come. And there's always plenty to do."

"True. But I don't like the insomnia." He walked across to her. "You and I need a rest. When the job's finished, we're both going to have one. Shall I tell you something? I'm at it early myself because I mean to finish by Friday night so that we both have a carefree week-end."

He patted her shoulder and turned away. Pulling out a keyring, he went over to the big safe.

"Dr. Craig."

"Yes?" He glanced back.

"I suppose you will think it is none of my business,

but I feel"—she hesitated—"there are . . . dangers."

Craig faced her. The boyish gaiety became disturbed.

"What sort of dangers?"

Camille met his glance gravely, and he thought her eyes were glorious.

"You have invented something which many people—people capable of any outrage—want to steal from you. And sometimes I think you are very careless."

"In what way?"

"Well"—she lowered her eyes, for Craig's regard was becoming ardent—"I knew Sir Denis Nayland Smith's reputation. I expect he came here to tell you the same thing."

"So what?"

"There are precautions which you neglect."

"Tell me one."

"The safe combination is one. Do you ever change it?"

Craig smiled. "No," he confessed. "Why should I? Nobody else knows it."

"How can you be sure?"

"Sam might have picked it up—so might you. But why worry?"

"I may be foolish. But even if only Sam and I knew it, in your place I should change it, Dr. Craig."

Craig stared. His expression conveyed nothing definite, but it embarrassed her.

"Not suggesting that Sam—"

"Of course not! I'm only suggesting that, for all our sakes, nobody but yourself should know that combination."

Craig brushed his hair back and began to grope in a pocket for cigarettes.

"Point begins to dawn, vaguely," he said. "Rather cloudy morning, but promise of a bright day. You mean that if something should be pinched therefrom, it must be clear that neither you nor Sam could possibly have known how to open the safe?"

"Yes," said Camille, "I suppose that is what I mean."

Craig stood there watching her door for some time after she had gone in and closed it. Then, he crossed, slowly, to the safe.

He had come to the conclusion that Camille was as clever as she was beautiful. He could not know that she had forced herself to this decision to warn him only after many sleepless hours.

Having arranged his work to his satisfaction, Craig took up the phone and dialled a number. When he got through:

"Please connect me with Sir Denis Nayland Smith," he said.

There was an interval, and then the girl at the hotel switchboard reported, "There's no reply from his apartment."

"Oh—well, would you give him a message to call Dr. Morris Craig when he comes in."

As he hung up he was thinking that Smith was early afoot. He had seen nothing of him since they had dined together, and was burning with anxiety on his behalf. The delicate instrument which Craig called a transmuter had already gone into construction. Shaw was working on a blueprint in the laboratory. It remained only for Craig to complete three details, and for tests to discover whether his plant could control the power he had invoked.

In view of what failure might mean, he had determined to insist that the entire equipment be moved, secretly, to a selected and guarded site in the open country for the carrying out of these tests.

He was beginning to realize that the transmuter might burst under the enormous load of energy it was designed to distribute. If it did, not only the Huston Building but also a great part of neighboring Manhattan could be dispersed like that lump of steel he had used in a demonstration for Nayland Smith.

Craig, in fact, was victim of an odd feeling of unrest. He continued to discount Smith's more dramatic warnings, and this in spite of the murderous attempt on Moreno, but he was unsure of the future. The feathered dart he had sent to Professor White at Harvard for examination, but so far had had no report.

He pressed a button, then sat on a corner of the desk, swinging one leg, as Sam came in, chewing industriously.

"Morning, boss."

"Good morning, Sam. What time do you turn up here as a rule?"

"Well"—Sam shook his head thoughtfully—"I'm mostly around by eight, on account of Mr. Shaw or Mr. Regan come off night watch then. I might easy be wanted—see?"

"Yes, I see. Reason I ask is I thought I saw you tailing me as I came along. If this impression was chimerical, correct me. But it isn't the first time I have had it."

95

Sam's eyes, behind his spectacles, betrayed childish wonder.

"*Me* tail *you*, Doctor! Listen. Wait a minute—"

"I am listening, and I am prepared to wait a minute. But I want an answer."

"Well,"—Sam pulled his eye-shade lower—"sometimes it happens maybe I'm on an errand same time you happen to be going my way—"

"Enough! I understand. You are my Old Man of the Sea, kindly supplied by Nayland Smith. If Mr. Frobisher knew how you wasted time you owe to Huston Electric, he'd fire you. But I'll have it out with Smith, when I see him."

A curious expression crossed Sam's face as Craig spoke, but was gone so quickly that, turning away, he didn't detect it.

As Sam went out, Craig stood studying the detail on the drawing board, but found himself unable to conquer that spirit of unrest, an unhealthy sense of impending harm, which had descended upon him. Particularly, he was troubled by forebodings about Smith. And although Morris Craig would have rejected such a theory with scientific scorn, it is nevertheless possible that these were telepathic . . .

Less than nine hours before, police headquarters had become a Vesuvius.

Nayland Smith's wallet had been handed in by the frightened patrolman to whom he had passed it. He had given a detailed description of the man posing as "Dr. Malcolm." It was recognized, at Centre Street, to correspond to that of the bogus doctor who had saved the life of Officer Moreno!

Wires had hummed all night. The deputy commis-

sioner had been called at his home. So had the
district attorney. All cars in the suspected area were
radioed. Senior police officers took charge of operations. What had been regarded, in certain quarters, as
an outbreak of hysteria in the F.B.I. suddenly crystal-
lized into a present menace, when the news broke that
a celebrated London consultant had been swept off
the map of Manhattan.

From the time that "Dr. Malcolm" had left with his
supposed patient, nothing more was known of his
movements. His identity remained a mystery. Feverish
activity prevailed. But not a solitary clue came in.

An internationally famous criminal investigator
had been spirited away under the very eyes of the
police — and no one knew where to look for him!

But Manhattan danced on . . .

Craig's uneasiness grew greater as the day grew
older. It began seriously to interfere with concentration. His lunch consisted of a club sandwich and a
bottle of beer sent up from the restaurant on the main
floor, below. The nearer that Shaw's work came to
completion in the laboratory, the further Craig
seemed to be from contributing those final elements
which would give it life. The more feverishly he toiled
the less he accomplished.

Early in the afternoon he spoke to the manager of
Nayland Smith's hotel.

He learned that Smith had gone out, the evening
before, at what exact time the manager didn't know.
He had not returned nor communicated. There had
been many callers, and a quantity of messages, mail,

and cables awaited him. The manager could give no further information.

Craig wondered if he should call police headquarters, but hesitated to make himself a nuisance. After all, the nature of Smith's business in New York would sufficiently account for long absences. But Craig recalled, unhappily, something he had said on the night they dined together: "I fear that he" (Dr. Fu Manchu) "has decided that I must die . . . What are my chances?"

He tried again to tackle his work, but found the problems which it presented so bewildering that he was not resentful, rather grateful, when Michael Frobisher burst into the office.

"Hullo, Mr. Frobisher!"

Craig swung around and faced his chief, who had dropped into one of the armchairs.

"Hello, Craig. Thought I'd just look in. Don't expect to be in town again this week. Picking up Mrs. F., who's having a treatment, and driving right out. How's the big job shaping?"

Frobisher pulled a cigar from his breast pocket, and Craig noted that his hand was unsteady. The florid coloring had undertones of grey. Sudden recognition came to him that Frobisher was either a sick man or a haunted one.

"Fairly bright," he replied in his most airy manner. "Time you saw the setup in the lab again."

"Yes—I must."

But Craig knew that he would avoid the visit, if possible. The throbbing monster which had its being in the laboratory frightened Michael Frobisher, a fact of which Craig was aware.

"Getting quite a big boy now."

Frobisher snipped off the end of his cigar. "What are the prospects of finishing by week-end?"

"Fair to medium. Mental functions disturbed by grave misgivings."

Frobisher glanced up sharply. His eyes, under drawn black brows, reminded Craig, for some reason, of smouldering fires in two deep caves.

"What misgivings?" he growled, and snapped-up his lighter, which had a flame like a burning oil well.

Craig, facing Frobisher, dropped the stub of a cigarette and began to grope behind him for a packet which he had put somewhere on the desk.

"I'm a sort of modern Frankenstein," he explained. "Hadn't grasped it before, but see it now. In there" — he waved towards the laboratory door — "is a pup of a thing which, full grown, could eat up New York City at one gulp. This brute frightens me."

"Forget it." Frobisher lighted his cigar.

"Imposs. The thought hangs on like a bulldog. How this beast can be tamed to perform domestic duties escapes me at the moment. Like training a Bengal tiger to rock baby's cradle. Then, there's something else."

"Such as what?"

"My love child, the horror begotten in that laboratory, is coveted by the governments of the United States, of England, and of Russia."

Michael Frobisher stood up. His craggy brows struggled to meet over a deep vertical wrinkle.

"Who says so?"

"I say so. Agents of all those governments are watching every move we make here."

"I knew there was a leak! Do you know those agents?"

"Sir Denis Nayland Smith has arrived from London."

"Who in hell is Sir Denis Nayland Smith?"

"An old friend of mine. Formerly a commissioner of Scotland Yard. But I don't know the Washington agent and I don't know the Soviet agent. I only know they're here."

"Oh!" said Michael Frobisher, and sat down again. "Any more troubles?"

"Yes." Craig found his cigarettes and lighted one. "Dr. Fu Manchu."

Silence fell between them like a curtain. Craig had turned again to the desk. He swung back now, and glanced at Frobisher. His expression was complicated. But fear was in it. He looked up at Craig.

"You are sure there *is* such a person?"

"Yes—moderately sure."

For some reason this assurance seemed to bring relief to Frobisher. A moment later an explanation came.

"Then I'm not crazy—as that damned Pardoe thinks! Those Asiatic snoopers really exist. They seem to have quit tailing me around town, but queer things happen out at Falling Waters. Whoever went through my papers one night away back must have been working with inside help—"

"But I thought you told me that some yellow character—"

"*He* was outside. Saw him from my dressing-room window. No locks broken. Then, only last night, my private safe was opened!"

100

"What's that?"

"Plain fact. I was awake. Sleep badly. Guess I interrupted him. But the door of the safe was wide open when I got down!"

"See anybody?"

"Not a one. Nothing taken. Doors and windows secure. Craig"—Frobisher's deep voice faltered—"I was beginning to wonder—"

"If you walked in your sleep? Did these things yourself?"

"Well—"

"Quite understand, and sympathize."

Michael Frobisher executed a shaking movement with his head, rather like that of a big dog who has something in his ear.

"Listen—but not a word to Mrs. F. I have had a gadget fixed up to record any movement around the house, and show just where it's coming from. I want you to look it over this weekend."

"Delightful prospect. I am the gadget king. And this brings me to my main misgiving. You may recall the bother we had fitting up the plant in the lab?"

"Don't be funny! Didn't we import workmen from Europe to make it in sections—"

"We did. And I have been my own draughtsman."

"Then send 'em home again and assemble the sections ourselves?"

" 'Ourselves' relating to Shaw, Regan and me? I fail to recall any instance when you put your Herculean but dignified shoulder to the wheel. Still, you were highly encouragin'. Yes—well—to be brief, we shall have to do likewise once more."

"What's that?"

"I cannot be responsible for tests carried out in the heart of New York City. Some of my experiments already are slightly alarming. But when I'm all set to tap the juice in quantities, I want to be where I can do no harm." Craig was warming to his subject; the enthusiasm of the specialist fired his eyes. "You see, the energy lies in successive strata—like the skins of an onion. And you know what the middle of a raw onion's like!"

The tip of Frobisher's cigar glowed ominously.

"Conveying what?" he growled through closed lips.

"Conveying that a site must be picked for an experimental station. Somewhere in wide-open spaces, far from the madding crowd. Little by little and bit by bit we shall transfer our monster there."

"You told me you needed some high place."

"There are high places other than the top of the Huston Building. I wish to avoid repeating, in the Huston Building, the story of the Tower of Babel. It would be spectacular, but unpopular."

Michael Frobisher got up, crossed, removed the cigar from his lips, and stood right in front of Craig.

"Listen. You're not getting cold feet, are you?"

Craig smiled, that slightly mischievous, schoolboy smile which was so irresistibly charming.

"Yes," he said. "I am. What are you going to do about it?"

Michael Frobisher turned and picked up his hat, which he had dropped on the floor beside his chair.

"If *you* say so, I'll have to get busy." He glanced at his wrist watch. "Give me all the facts on Saturday."

When Frobisher opened the office door, he stood looking to right and left of the lobby for a moment before he went out.

Craig scratched his chin reflectively. What, exactly, was going on at Falling Waters? He felt peculiarly disinclined to work, considered ringing for Camille, not because he required her attendance, but for the pure pleasure of looking at her, then resolutely put on his glasses and settled down before the problem symbolized by that unfinished diagram.

He was destined, however, to be interrupted again.

The office door behind him opened very quietly, and Mrs. Frobisher peeped in. Craig remained unaware of her presence.

"Do I intrude?" she asked coyly.

Craig, conscious of shirt-sleeves, took off his glasses, jumped from the stool, and turned.

"Why—Mrs. Frobisher!" He swept back the drooping forelock. "I say, excuse my exposed laundry."

Stella Frobisher extended her hand graciously. She didn't offer it; she extended it. She was an Englishwoman and her pattern of life appeared to be modelled upon customs embalmed in old volumes of *Punch*. Her hair had been blond, and would always remain so. She had canarylike manners. She fluttered.

"I was waiting until Mike had gone. He mustn't *know* I have been here."

Craig pulled a chair forward, and Stella Frobisher's high heels clicked like castanets on the parquet as she crossed and sat down. She was correctly dressed in full mink uniform and wore a bird of paradise for a hat.

"Highly compromising. When did your heart first awaken to my charms?" said Craig as he put his coat on.

He had learned that airy badinage was the only possible kind of conversation with Mrs. Frobisher, who was some years younger than her husband and liked to think he had many rivals.

"Oh, you *do* say the queerest things!" Stella's reputation for vivacity rested largely upon her habit of stressing words at random. "I have been having a *treatment* at Professor Hoffmeyer's."

"Am I acquainted with the lad?"

"Oh, *everybody* knows him. He's *simply* too wonderful. He has made a *new* woman of me."

"Yes. You look quite new."

"Oh, now you think I'm being silly, Dr. Craig. But truly my *nerves* had quite gone. You see, there's something *very* queer going on."

"Queer goings on, eh?" Craig murmured, hunting for his cigarettes.

"*Most* peculiar. I know you're *laughing* at me. But truly I'm terrified. There have been the *most* uncanny people prowling about Falling Waters recently." She accepted a cigarette and Craig lighted it for her. "I simply *dare* not *speak* to Mike about it. You know how nervous he is. But I have ordered a *pack* of Alsatians from Wanamaker's or *somewhere* and insisted they *must* be ferocious."

"A pack, you say?"

"A pack," Stella repeated firmly. "I don't know how many *dogs* there are in a pack, but I *suppose* fifty-two."

"Expect the pack this week-end?"

"I *hope* so. Of course, I have engaged a *special* man to look after them."

"Of course. Lion tamer, or some such character."

"I have had barbed *wire* installed, and I shall *loose* the dogs at night."

"Sounds uncommonly attractive. Lovers' paradise."

"I wanted to *warn* you, because now I must be *off*. If I'm late at the Ritz, Mike will think I've been *up* to something—"

Craig escorted her down to the street and was rewarded with an arch smile. Stella's smile was an heirloom which had probably belonged to her mother.

chapter 9

Nayland Smith came to the surface from depths of an unfathomable purple lake. A voice, unpleasantly familiar, matter-of-fact, reached his ears through violet haze which overhung the lake.

"I trust you find yourself quite restored, Sir Denis?"

Smith strove to identify the speaker; to determine his true environment; to find himself.

"And don't hesitate to reply. You are no longer dumb. The discomfort was temporary."

The speaker was identified. He was Dr. Malcolm!

"I—I—why . . . thank God! I can *speak*!"

Nayland Smith's voice rose higher on every word.

"So I observe. You are an expert boxer, Sir Denis; for a man of your years a remarkable one. Myself, although trained in several types of wrestling, unfortunately I know little of boxing."

Dr. Malcolm wore a long white coat. He was regarding Smith with professional interest.

"Too bad. You'll miss it when I get loose!" Smith rapped.

But Dr. Malcolm retained his suavity.

"Pugnacity highly developed. You appear to feel no gratitude for your restored power of speech?"

He poured a vivid blue liquid from a beaker into a phial. The phial he placed in a leather case.

"No. I'm waiting for the later symptoms to develop."

Dr. Malcolm reclosed his case.

"You will wait in vain. The first injection I administered was intended merely to paralyze the muscles of articulation."

"Thanks. It did."

"A second counteracted it."

"Truly ingenious."

"But," Dr. Malcolm went on, "my duties in your case were not nearly so dangerous as in the case of the policeman, Moreno. I was subject to exposure throughout the time I remained in the hospital."

"So I gather," said Smith.

This man's cool audacity fascinated him.

"Of course"—Dr. Malcolm locked his leather case—"Circle 7-0300 is the number of a well-known hotel. I don't live there." He showed strong white teeth in a smile. "Mai Cha was most convincing as the girl who had been robbed, I thought?"

"I thought so too."

Nayland Smith glanced about him. The place proved to be more extensive than he had supposed at that strange awakening. It was a big cellar. Much of it was unlighted—a dim background of mystery.

"We had several key men in the crowd, of course. The police officer was an intruder. But I did my best with him."

("So did I!" Nayland Smith was thinking.)

"When you succeeded in knocking me out, I was indebted to this officer—and to a pair of our people placed to cover such a possibility — for your recapture."

"Yes, you were," said Smith conversationally. "All the luck lay with you." As Dr. Malcolm picked up his case: "Must you be going?"

"Yes. I am leaving you now. I regret the incivility of putting you under constraint. You will have noted, since you are fully restored, that your arms are lightly attached to the bench upon which you sit. These thin lines, however, are quite unbreakable, except by a wire-cutter. A preparation invented by my principal. I bid you good night, Sir Denis. It is improbable that we meet again."

"Highly improbable," Smith murmured. "But lucky, once more, for you! By the way, how long have I been here?"

Dr. Malcolm paused.

"Nearly twenty-four hours —"

"What!"

"Not actually in this cellar, but under my care, elsewhere. You have been suitably nourished, and I assure you there will be no ill effects."

Dr. Malcolm merged into the background. His white coat, ghostlike, marked his progress for a while and then became swallowed up. An evidently heavy door was opened — and closed.

Twenty-four hours!

Nayland Smith satisfied himself that he was indeed helpless. The slender, flexible threads, like strands of silk, which confined his arms were steel-tough. The bench was clamped to the floor. He peered into surrounding gloom. One light on the wall behind him afforded sole illumination. Outside its radius lay shadows ever increasing to complete blackness.

Somewhere in this blackness, almost defying scrutiny, objects were stacked against a further wall. Specks of color became discernible, vague forms.

Intently Smith stared into the darkness, picking out shapes, dim lines.

At last he understood.

He was looking at a pile of Chinese coffins . . .

The sound made by a heavy, unseen door warned him of the fact that someone had entered the cellar.

Long before a tall figure came silently out of the shadows, Nayland Smith knew who had entered. The quality of the atmosphere had changed, become charged with new portent.

Wearing a dark, fur-collared topcoat and carrying a black hat in one long, yellow hand, Nayland Smith's ancient adversary faced him.

A tense, silent moment passed.

"I confess that I had not expected to meet you, Sir Denis."

The words were spoken softly, the sibilants marked.

Nayland Smith met the regard of half-closed eyes.

"I, on the contrary, had hoped to meet *you*, Dr. Fu Manchu."

"Your star above mine. The meeting has taken place. If it is not as you had foreseen it, blame only that blind Fate which disturbs our foolish plans. Because our destinies were woven on the same loom, perhaps I should have known that you would be here—to obstruct me when the survival of mankind is at stake."

He stepped aside, and brought a rough wooden box. Upon this he sat down.

"You are compelled to remain seated," he explained. "Courtesy forbids me to stand."

And those words were a key to open memory's door. Nayland Smith, in one magical glimpse, lived again through a hundred meetings with Dr. Fu Manchu, through years in which he had labored to rid the world of this insane genius. He saw him as an assassin, as a torturer, as the most dangerous criminal the law had ever known; but always as an aristocrat.

"You honor me," he said drily. "How am I to die?"

Dr. Fu Manchu fully opened his strange eyes and fixed a gaze upon Smith which few men could have hoped to sustain.

"That rests with you, Sir Denis," he replied, and spoke even more softly than he had spoken before.

It is at least possible that the disappearance of Nayland Smith might have gone onto the unsolved list if any detective officer other than George Moreno (already back on duty) had been assigned to a certain post that night.

The shop of Huan Tsung, for which Smith had set out the night before, was being kept under routine observation. And at ten o'clock Moreno relieved a man who had been on duty since six. Chinatown was Moreno's special stamping-ground, and his orders were to make a record of all visitors and to note particularly any movements of the mysterious proprietor.

The small and stuffy room from which he operated put up a blend of odors uniquely sick-making. It was one of several in the house commanding an excellent

110

view of part of the Asiatic quarter, and this was not the first time it had been used for police surveillance. But the dangerous days of tong wars seemed to be over. Chinatown was as gently mannered as Park Avenue.

He had been there for a long time when old Huan Tsung's antique Ford was brought around to the front of the shop. Assisted by a yellow-complexioned driver of ambiguous nationality, and a spruce young shopman, the aged figure came out and entered the car. Huan Tsung wore a heavy, dark topcoat with a fur collar; the wide brim of a soft black hat half concealed his features. His eyes were protected by owlish spectacles.

The Ford was driven off. The shopman returned to the shop.

Moreno knew that the journey would be kept under observation. But he doubted if any evidence of value would result. In all likelihood, these drives were purely constitutional. The old man believed in the merit of night air.

After his departure, little more occurred for some time. Chinatown displayed a deadly respectability. Moreno, who had a pair of powerful glasses, began to grow restive. He learned that he could read even the smaller lettering on shop signs across the street. Faces of passers-by might be inspected minutely. But no one of particular interest came within range of the Zeiss lenses.

There were callers at Huan Tsung's, Asiatic and Occidental, some, at least, legitimate customers; but none to excite suspicion . . .

A small truck drew up before the shop. The young

Oriental opened a cellar trap and assisted a truckman to lower a big packing-case covered with Chinese lettering into the basement.

Evidently a consignment of goods of some kind. Moreno wondered vaguely what kind. Something uncommonly heavy.

The trap was reclosed. The truck went away.

Moreno, in the airless room, began to grow sleepy. Then, in a flash, he was wide awake.

A tall man had just come out of Huan Tsung's. He wore a dark topcoat, a white scarf, and a neat black hat. He carried a leather case. Moreno, in the first place, hadn't seen this man go in; therefore he instantly focussed the glasses on his face. And, as he did so, his hands shook slightly.

It was the first face he had seen when he had opened his eyes in the hospital.

The man was "Dr. Malcolm"!

Moreno was hurrying downstairs when Huan Tsung's time-honored Ford returned, and the shopman came out to aid a dark-coated figure to alight. It had been driven away before Moreno reached the street — and Dr. Malcolm had disappeared.

"My mission," said Fu Manchu, "is to save the world from the leprosy of Communism. Only I can do this. And I do it, not because of any love I have for the American people, but because if the United States fall, the whole world falls. In this task, Sir Denis, I shall brook no interference."

Nayland Smith made no reply. He was listening, not only to the sibilant, incisive voice, but also to certain vague sounds which penetrated the cellar. He was trying to work out where the place was located.

"Morris Craig, a physicist touched with genius, is perfecting a device which, in the hands of warmongers, would wreck those fragments of civilization which survive the maniac, Hitler. News of this pending disaster brought me here. I am inadequately served. There has been no time to organize a suitable staff. My aims you know."

Nayland Smith nodded. From faint sounds detected, he had deduced the fact that the cellar lay near a busy street.

"I appreciate your aims. I don't like your methods."

"We shall not discuss them. They are effective. Your recent visit to Teheran (I regret that I missed you there) failed to save Omar Khan. He was the principal Soviet agent in that area. Power is strong wine even for men of culture. When it touches the lips of those unaccustomed to it, power drives them mad. Such a group of power-drunk fools threaten today the future of man. One of its agents is watching Craig's experiments. He must be silenced."

"Why don't you silence him?"

The brilliant green eyes almost closed, so that they became mere slits in an ivory mask. It is possible that Nayland Smith was the only man of his acquaintance who assumed, although he didn't feel, complete indifference in the presence of Dr. Fu Manchu.

"I have always respected your character, Sir Denis." The words were no more than whispered. "It has that mulish stupidity which won the Battle of Britain. The incompetents who serve me have failed, so far, to identify this agent. I still believe that if you could

113

appreciate my purpose, you would become of real use to a world hurtling headlong to disaster. I repeat — I respect your character."

"It was this respect, no doubt, which prompted you to attempt my murder?"

"The attempt was clumsy. It was undertaken contrary to my wishes. You can be of greater use to me alive than dead."

And those softly spoken words were more terrifying to Nayland Smith than any threat.

Had Fu Manchu decided to smuggle him into his far eastern base, by that mysterious subway which so far had defied all inquiry?

As the dreadful prospect flashed to his mind, Fu Manchu exercised one of his many uncanny gifts, that of answering an unspoken question.

"Yes — such is my present intention, Sir Denis. I have work for you to do. This cellar is shared by several Asiatic tradesmen, one of whom is an importer of Chinese coffins. A death has occurred in the district, and the deceased — a man of means — expressed a wish to be buried in his birthplace. When his coffin is sent there, via Hong Kong — he will not be in it . . ."

There was an interruption.

Heralded by the sound of an opening door, two stockily built, swarthy figures entered. One of them limped badly. Between them they carried an ornate coffin. This they set down on the concrete floor, and saluted Dr. Fu Manchu profoundly.

Nayland Smith clenched his fists, straining, briefly but uselessly, at the slender, remorseless strands which held him. The men were Burmese ruffians of the dacoit class from which Fu Manchu had formerly recruited his bodyguard. One of them—the one who limped and who had a vicious cast in his right eye—spoke rapidly.

Fu Manchu silenced him with a gesture. But Nayland Smith had heard—and understood. His heart leapt. Hope was reborn. But Fu Manchu remained unmoved. He spoke calmly.

"The preparation for your long journey," he said, "is one calling for time and care. It must be postponed. In the past, I believe, you have had opportunities to study examples of that synthetic death (a form of catalepsy) which I can induce. I hope to operate in the morning. This"—he extended a long-nailed forefinger in the direction of the coffin—"will be your *wagon-lit*. You will require no passport . . ."

Nayland Smith detected signs of uneasiness in the two Burmese. The one who limped and squinted was watching him murderously—for this was the man upon whom he had registered a kick the night before. Faintly he could hear sounds of passing traffic, but nothing else. The odds against his survival were high.

Dr. Fu Manchu signalled again—and the two Burmese stepped forward to where the helpless prisoner sat watching them . . .

The life of Chinatown apparently pursued its normal midnight course. Smartly dressed Orientals, inscrutably reserved, passed along the streets, as well as less smartly dressed Westerners. Some of the shops and restaurants continued to do business. Others were closing. There was nothing to indicate that

Chinatown was covered, that every man and woman leaving it did so under expert scrutiny.

"If Nayland Smith's here," said the grim deputy commissioner, who had arrived to direct operations in person, "they won't get him out—alive or dead."

He spoke with the full knowledge which experience had given him, that practically every inhabitant knew that a cordon had been thrown around the whole area.

When Police Captain Rafferty walked into Huan Tsung's shop, he found a young Oriental there, writing by the poor light of a paper-shaded lamp. He glanced up at Rafferty without apparent interest.

"Where's Huan Tsung?"

"Not home."

"Where's he gone?"

"Don't know."

"When did he go?"

"Ten minute—quarter hour."

This confirmed reports. The Ford exhibit had appeared again. Old Huan Tsung had sallied forth a second time.

"When's he coming back?"

"Don't know."

"Suppose you try a guess, Charlie. Expect him tonight?"

"Sure."

The shopman resumed his writing.

"While we're waiting," said Police Captain Rafferty, "we'll take a look around. Lead the way upstairs. You can finish that ballad when we come down."

The young shopman offered no protest. He put his

brush away and stood up.

"If you please," he said, and opened a narrow door at the back of the counter.

At about the time that Rafferty started upstairs, a radio message came through to the car which served the deputy commissioner as mobile headquarters. It stated that Huan Tsung's vintage Ford was parked on lower Fifth Avenue just above Washington Square.

Inquiries brought to light the fact that it stood before an old brick house. The officer reporting didn't know who occupied this house. Huan Tsung had called there earlier that night and had returned to Pell Street. He was now presumably there again.

"Do I go in and get him?" the officer inquired.

"No. But keep him covered when he comes out."

This order of the deputy commissioner's was one of those strategic blunders which have sometimes lost wars . . .

Police Captain Raffety found little of note in the rooms above the shop. They resembled hundreds of such apartments to be seen in that neighbourhood. The sanctum of Huan Tsung, with its silk-covered walls and charcoal brazier, arrested his attention for a while. At the crystal globe he stared with particular interest, then glanced at his guide, whose name (or so he said) was Lao Tai.

"Fortuneteller work here?"

Lao Tai shook his head.

"Here Huan Tsung meditate. Huan Tsung great thinker."

"He'll have to think fast tonight. You have a cellar down below. Show me the way in."

Lao Tai obeyed, leading Rafferty through to the

back of the shop where a narrow wooden stair was almost hidden behind piles of merchandise. He switched up a light at the bottom of the stair and Rafferty went clattering down.

He found himself in a cellar not much greater in area than the shop above. A chute communicated with a trap in the sidewalk overhead. Cartons and crates bearing Chinese labels and lettering nearly filled the place. It smelled strongly of spice and rotten fish.

One long, narrow packing-case seemed to have been recently opened. Rafferty examined it with some care, then turned to Lao Tai, who watched him disinterestedly.

"When did this thing come?"

"Come tonight."

Rafferty was beginning to wonder. All this man's answers added up correctly — for he knew that such a crate had been delivered earlier that night.

"What was in it?"

"This and that."

Lao Tai vaguely indicated the litter around.

"Well, show me some 'this.' Then we can take a look at any 'that' you've got handy."

Lao Tai touched a chest of tea with a glossily disdainful shoe, and pointed to a number of bronze bowls stacked up on a rough wooden bench. His slightly slanting eyes held no message but one of a boredom too deep for expression. And it was while Police Captain Rafferty was wondering what lay hidden under this crust and how to break through to it, that Huan Tsung's remarkable chariot returned to Pell Street and the old man was helped out.

He expressed neither surprise nor interest at finding police on the premises. He bowed courteously when Raymond Harkness stated that he had some questions to put to him, and, leaning on the arm of his Mongolian driver, led the way upstairs. Seating himself on the cushioned divan in the silk-lined room, he dismissed the driver, offered cigarettes, and suggested tea.

"Thanks—no," said Harkness in his quiet way. "Just a few questions. You are acquainted with a doctor; a European, I believe. He is tall, dark, and wears a slight moustache. He called here tonight. I should be glad of his address."

Huan Tsung began to fill a long-stemmed pipe. He had extraordinarily slender, adroit fingers.

"I fear I cannot help you," he replied in his courteous, exact English. "A European physician, you say?" He shook his head. "It is possible, if he came here, that he came only to make a purchase. Have you questioned my assistant?"

"I haven't. The man I mean is employed by Dr. Fu Manchu."

Not one of Huan Tsung's thousand wrinkles stirred. His benevolent gaze became fixed upon Harkness.

"A strange name," he murmured. "No doubt a *nom de guerre*. Tell me more of this strangely named doctor, if I am to help you."

"It's for you to tell *me* more. Will you tell me now, or will you come along and tell the boys at Centre Street?"

"Why, may I ask, should I drag my old bones to Centre Street?"

"It won't be necessary, if you care to talk. You are an educated man, and I'm prepared to treat you that way if you behave sensibly."

Huan Tsung went on filling his pipe. The illegible parchment of his features became creased by what might have been a smile.

"It is true. I formerly administered a large province of China, probably with justice, and certainly with success. Events, however, necessitated my departure without avoidable delay."

"Did you know Dr. Fu Manchu in China?"

Huan Tsung ignited a paper spill in the brazier and began to light his pipe.

"I regret deeply that your question is a foolish one. I thought I had made it clear that I am unacquainted with this person."

"Pity your memory's getting so unreliable," said Harkness.

"Alas, after seventy, each succeeding year robs us of a hundred delights."

Heavy footsteps sounded on the stairs, and Captain Rafferty came in.

"Listen—there's a door down in the basement leading to some other place—another cellar, I guess. Let's have the key, or shall I break it open?"

Huan Tsung regarded the intruder mildly.

"I fear you have no choice," he said. "The door leads, as you say, into the storeroom of my neighbor, Kwee Long, whose premises are on the adjoining street. He will have gone, no doubt. The door is locked from the other side. I possess no key to this door."

"Sure of that, Huan Tsung?" Harkness asked

quietly.

"Unless my failing memory betrays me."

The door in the cellar was forced. It proved no easy job: it was a strong, heavy door. The police found themselves in a much larger cellar, which evidently ran under several stores and was of irregular shape. Part of it seemed to be used by a caterer, for there were numerous cases of imported delicacies. They could find no switches and worked by the light of their lamps.

Then they came to the part where Chinese coffins were stacked.

This place struck a chill—to the spirit as well as to the body. The deputy commissioner had just joined the party. Their only clues, so far, led to Huan Tsung's. Hope rested on the report of Officer Moreno, that the pseudo-doctor had been seen leaving there that night.

"No evidence anybody's been around here," Rafferty declared. "See any more doors any place?"

"There's one over here, Captain," came a muffled voice.

All flocked in that direction. Sure enough, there was, at the back of a deep alcove. The man who had found it tried to open it. He had no success.

"Smash it!" the deputy commissioner ordered.

And they had just gone to work with that enthusiasm which such an order always inspires, when Rafferty held his hand up.

"Quiet, everybody!"

Nervous silence succeeded clamor.

"What did you think you heard?" a hoarse whisper came from the deputy commissioner.

"Sort of tapping, sir."

A silent interval of listening in semidarkness; then another whisper:

"Where from?"

"The coffins . . . Ssh! There it is again!"

Another pause for listening followed, in which the rays of more than one flashlamp moved unsteadily.

"Maybe there's a rat in there."

"Quiet! Listen!"

A faint, irregular knocking sound became audible. It was followed by one which resembled a stifled moan.

"Quick! This way! Open all those things. Down with the lot!"

A rush back to the coffin cellar took place. They pulled down five or six, and found them empty. Rafferty held up his hand.

"Stop the clatter. Listen."

All became quiet. And from somewhere near the base of another pile not yet attacked they heard it again, more clearly . . . tapping and a stifled groan.

"It's that thing with all the gilt! Last but one from the floor!"

They went to work with a will. To move the empty coffins on top was a business of minutes. And in the most ornate specimen of all, they found Nayland Smith.

His wrists and ankles were lashed up with what looked like sewing silk. But clasp-knives failed to cut it. A piece of surgical strapping was fastened across his mouth. When this had been removed:

"Thank God you heard me," he croaked. "I could just move one foot. Don't blunt your knives on this stuff. Get a wire-cutter. Lift me out."

Two men lifted him out, and supported him to a bench set before the opposite wall. He smiled grimly as he sat there. The deputy commissioner produced a flask.

"Thank God indeed, Sir Denis. It's a miracle you weren't suffocated."

"Air holes bored in coffin. Never mind *me*. What of Dr. Fu Manchu?"

"Not a sign of him."

Nayland Smith sighed, and took a drink.

"Yet he left here little more than half an hour ago."

"*What!* But it's impossible! No one has left this area during that time who wasn't known to be a regular resident."

Smith shot him a steely glance.

"What about Huan Tsung? Doesn't he wear a wide-brimmed hat and a heavy, fur-lined coat?"

The deputy commissioner and Captain Rafferty exchanged worried looks.

"He does, and he certainly went out again," said Rafferty. "He went twice to a house on lower Fifth. But he's back."

"He may be," Smith rapped. "But he only went there once. It was Dr. Fu Manchu, dressed like him, who came back and Dr. Fu Manchu who has just slipped through your fingers again! Have this Fifth Avenue place raided—*now* . . . But already it's too late."

chapter 10

Manhattan danced on tirelessly: a city of a thousand jewelled minarets, and not one mueddin to call Manhattan to prayer.

An enemy, one who aspired to nothing less than dictatorship of the United States, was within the gates, watching Morris Craig's revolutionary experiments. London, knowing the hazard, watched also. Washington, alive to the menace, had instructed the F.B.I. And the F.B.I., smelling out the presence of a further danger, in the formidable person of Dr. Fu Manchu, had sent for Nayland Smith.

But no hint of the desperate battle waging in their midst was permitted to reach the ears of those whose fate hung in the balance. That hapless unit, the Man in the Street, went about his affairs never suspecting that a third world war raged on his doorstep.

Nayland Smith called up Craig the next morning.

"Thought you might be worried," he said. "Had a bit of a brush with the enemy, but no bones broken. Watch your step, Craig. This thing is coming to a head. Hope to look in later . . ."

The mantle of gloom which had enveloped Craig

dropped from his shoulders. His problems no longer seemed insuperable. Clearly enough, opposition more dangerous than that of commercial rivalry was in the field against Huston Electric. His science-trained brain, which demanded tangible evidence before granting even trivial surmises, had fought against acceptance, not merely of the presence, but of the existence, of Dr. Fu Manchu.

Now he was converted.

Ignorant, yet, of what had happened to Nayland Smith, he must regard the attempt on Moreno as the work of some enemy unusually equipped. The mode of attack certainly suggested oriental influence.

If, then, Dr. Fu Manchu, what of the Soviet agent?

He might reasonably suppose, although Smith had never even hinted it, that Smith acted for the British government. Very well. Who was acting for the Kremlin?

Certainly, his discovery (for which, in his modest way, Craig claimed no personal credit) had called down the lightning. But, in his new mood, there was no place for misgiving. On the contrary, he was exultant; for by that night, he believed his task would be completed.

When Camille came in, he turned to her with a happy smile.

"Just heard from Nayland Smith. Thank heaven the old lad's okay."

"I am glad," said Camille, and Craig listened to the harp notes in her fascinating voice. "I know you were worried."

"I'm worried about you, too."

She started; her eyes seemed to assume a deeper

shade.

"Why—Dr. Craig?"

"You're overdoin' it, my dear. It simply won't work, you know. Because I'm sure you're not getting enough sleep."

"Do I look such a wreck?" she smiled.

"You always look lovely," he replied impulsively, and then regretted the words, for a faint flush tinged Camille's cheeks, and so he added, "when you don't wear those damned glasses."

"Oh!" said Camille—and he watched for, and saw, that adorable little *moue,* like a suppressed dimple, appear on her lip. "As you told me you didn't like them, I only wear them, now, when I am working."

"I didn't say anything of the kind. I said I preferred your eyes in the nude, so to speak. There's only one other thing you might do to add to my joy."

"What is that, Dr. Craig?"

"Well—must you hide the most wonderful hair that ever escaped captivity in Hollywood by pinning it behind your ears as if you wanted to forget it?"

Then Camille laughed, and her laughter rang true.

"Really, you *are* ridiculous! But very complimentary. You see, I know my hair is rather—well—flamboyant. It waves quite obstinately, and I don't feel—"

"It's a display entirely in order for the office of a stuffy physicist? Well—I'll let you off. But there's a proviso."

"What is the proviso, Dr. Craig?"

"That you unloose the latent fires as from tomorrow, when we disport ourselves at Falling Waters."

"Oh," said Camille demurely. "Am I allowed to

126

think it over?"

"Yes. But make up your mind by the morning."

Camille crossed toward the door of her room, then paused, and turned.

"I'm sorry. But I'm afraid I quite forgot to mention what I really came to ask you, Dr. Craig."

"Remembered now?"

"Yes. Mrs. Frobisher was speaking to me on the phone yesterday, and we discovered we both suffered from insomnia. She called me this morning to tell me she had arranged an appointment with Professor Hoffmeyer. Of course, I should never have dreamed of such a thing. But—"

"You can't duck it as the boss's wife has fixed it? Quite agree. He'll probably prescribe six weeks at Palm Beach. But pay no attention."

"What I wanted to ask you was if it would be all right for me to go along there at eight tonight?"

"Eight?"

"Yes. An unusual hour for a consultant. I suppose he is fitting me in when he has no other appointments."

"Between the cocktails and the soup, I should guess. Certainly, Miss Navarre. Why ask?"

"Well"—Camille hesitated—"I know you plan to work late tonight, and I'm often wanted to take notes—"

"Forget it. Proceed from the learned professor's straight to your sleeping-sack. We make an early start tomorrow morning."

"That's very kind of you, Dr. Craig, and I am grateful. But when I took this appointment I knew what the hours would be. I shall certainly come back."

Camille went into her room, quietly closing the door. All her movements were marked by a graceful composure.

At a quarter to eight, when Camille set out, Craig was crouched over his work, a formula like a Picasso landscape pinned to a corner of the board and a pen in his mouth.

"I expect to return in an hour, Dr. Craig."

Craig raised his hand in a gesture of dismissal and said something that might have been "Go to bed."

Camille pressed the button of the private elevator, and when it arrived, opened the door with her pass-key and went down to the thirty-second floor. She closed the door there—they were all self-locking—and crossed the big office, in which a light was always left on, to a similar door on the other side. She knew the second elevator would be below, for Regan had gone down at four o'clock, when Mr. Shaw had relieved him.

She pressed the button, and when the signal light glowed, unlocked the door and descended to the main floor. There was a small, dark lobby which opened directly onto the street, a means of private entry and exit used only by the laboratory and Michael Frobisher. At the moment that Camille stepped out of the elevator and as the door closed behind her, she knew that someone was in this lobby.

She stood quite still.

"Who's there?" she asked in a low voice.

"Don't be alarmed." A flashlamp came to life. "It's

128

only me—or I, if you're a purist!"

"Oh!" Camille whispered. "Sir Denis Nayland Smith—"

She could see his face now, framed in the upturned collar of a fur-lined coat. It was a very grim face.

"Wondering how I got in? Well, I'll explain the great illusion. I have a duplicate key! Craig up there?"

"Yes, Sir Denis—and very busy."

"Are you off for the night?"

"Not at all. I hope to be back in an hour."

"Good girl!" That revealing smile swept grimness from his face as swiftly as a mask removed. "I have excellent reports of your keenness and efficiency."

He patted her shoulder, passed her, and put his key in the elevator door.

Camille found herself standing on the street without quite knowing how she got there. Two men who gave her searching glances were lounging immediately outside, but, although her heart was racing, she preserved her admirable poise, waiting with apparent calm until a cruising taxi came along.

She gave the address, Woolton Building, and then tried to carry out advice printed on a card before her, "Sit back and relax."

Useless to ignore the fact that she had reached a climax in her affairs. The tangled threads of her existence had tripped her at almost every turn. True, she had snapped one. But Camille found herself thinking of Omar's words, "The Moving Finger writes; and, having writ—"

Morris must be told. She had made up her mind to tell him tomorrow. Her crowning dread was that he would find out from someone else. She wanted him

129

to learn the truth from her own lips . . .

Only one elevator remained in service at the Woolton Building. Most of the office staffs had left. Camille told the bored operator, "Professor Hoffmeyer."

"Hoffmeyer? Top."

She stepped out on an empty corridor. Directly facing her was a door marked, "Professor Hoffmeyer. Inquiries."

It proved to be a well-appointed reception office. No one was there.

Camille sat down on a cushioned divan. A clock above the desk told her that she was three minutes ahead of time. Morris's words flashed through her mind, "Between the cocktails and the soup."

On the stroke of eight, a Chinese girl came in through a doorway facing that by which visitors entered. She wore national dress and had a grace of movement which reminded Camille of a gazelle. Clasping her hands on her breast, she bowed.

"If you will be pleased to follow me," she said.

Camille followed her, across a large salon decorated with miniature reproductions of classic statuary and paintings of flawless nudity. There were richly cushioned settees, desks provided with the latest periodicals, softly shaded lamps. She began to understand that Professor Hoffmeyer was a luxury reserved for the wives and concubines of commercial sultans, and to wonder if Mrs. Frobisher had any idea of her salary.

From here they passed along a tiled corridor between cubicles resembling those in a Pompeian bath. There were medical odors mingling with all those perfumes peculiar to a beauty parlor.

There had been no one in the salon, and there was no one in any of the cubicles.

The journey ended in an office which, unlike the other apartments, conformed with Camille's idea of what a consultant's establishment should be. There was a large, neat desk. One of the drawers was open, as if someone had been seated there only a moment before. A number of scientific books filled a heavy mahogany case. On the right of this was an opening which evidently communicated with another room.

Camille's Chinese guide clasped her hands on her breast, bowed, and retired.

The place possessed a faint, sweetish smell. It awakened some dormant memory. Then a voice spoke, the voice of someone in the dimly lighted room beyond.

"Be so good as to enter."

Camille's mind, her spirit, rose in revolt. Suddenly she was fired by one impulse only—to escape. But she seemed to be incapable of attempting escape. Those words were a command she found herself helpless to disobey.

Slowly, with lagging steps, she walked in. Her movements made no sound on a thick carpet. It was an apartment Orientally furnished. There were arched openings in which lanterns hung. She saw painted screens, lacquer. But these were sketchy, a pencilled background for a figure seated behind a long, narrow table.

He wore a yellow robe; his chin rested on his hands, his elbows on the table. And his glittering green eyes claimed and owned her.

Camille stifled a scream, turned—and the opening through which she had come in was no longer there; only a beautifully wrought lacquer panel. She twisted back, fighting down hysteria. Her glance took in the whole room.

"Yes," the sibilant voice assured her, "you are not mistaken, Miss Navarre . . . you have been here before."

chapter 11

"The greatest compliment ever paid to me," said Nayland Smith grimly. "Dr. Fu Manchu considers I am more useful alive than dead!"

Morris Craig, seated, back to the desk, watched that lean, restless figure parading the office. Smith's hat and topcoat lay on the settee, his pipe bubbled between his small, even teeth. He looked gaunt, but his steps were springy, his eyes clear.

"I can only repeat — it's a miracle you're alive."

"I suppose it is. Mysterious news of the pending raid on Huan Tsung's led to a postponement of the treatment prescribed. Otherwise, I should have been found, certifiably dead, in that ghastly coffin. Failing the raid, I should by now be on my way to China."

"Do you think the headquarters of this thing are in China?"

"No," rapped Smith. "In Tibet. In a completely inaccessible spot. Lhasa is not the only secret city in Asia — nor Everest the highest mountain. But leave that. I want certain facts."

Craig lighted a cigarette which he had been holding for some time between his fingers.

"You shall have them. But there are certain facts I want, too. I'm not immune from human curiosity, even if I have harnessed a force new to physics. When the police found you last night, what about this fellow, Huan Tsung?"

Nayland Smith smiled. It was a smile of pure enjoyment. He pulled up, facing Craig.

"Huan Tsung, ex-governor of a Chinese province, and a prominent member of the Council of Seven, I had met before. He blandly denied any recollection of the meeting. As I had clearly been delivered at his shop during the evening in a crate, and taken into an adjoining cellar, Harkness and the commissioner proposed to arrest him."

"I should have proposed ditto."

"On what charge?" rapped Smith. "There are witnesses—including a police officer—to testify that he was not at home during the time I was being interviewed by Dr. Fu Manchu—"

"But you tell me he doubled with Fu Manchu—"

"Undoubtedly he did. But how can we prove it? A scholarly, elderly gentleman who claims to be French Canadian occupies the apartment on lower Fifth Avenue which Huan Tsung visited last night. They are old friends, it seems. They were discussing the political situation in China, and Huan Tsung returned to Pell Street for some correspondence bearing on the subject."

"But, Smith—you were found in his cellar!"

"It isn't his cellar, Craig. Remember, the police *broke* into it. And the man to whom it really belongs is out of town! Lastly, the shopman, a cultured liar, produced an invoice for the contents of the crate in which I was brought there from wherever I had been before!"

"But you say you recognized Huan Tsung?"

"Certainly. But he blandly assures me I am mistaken. He had the impudence to point out that to the Western eye, Chinese faces look much alike. Had he had the privilege of meeting me before, he said, such an honor couldn't possibly have escaped his memory!"

"Do you mean to say he's going to get away with it?"

"For the time being, I'm afraid he is. Mr. La Fosse of lower Fifth Avenue, who is undoubtedly in Fu Manchu's employ, declares that he never even heard of such a person. Of course, the police will watch them closely, as astronomers watch a new comet. Their lines are tapped already."

"And what about those damned injections? Do you feel no ill effects?"

"None whatever. You must accept the fact, Craig, that Dr. Fu Manchu has a knowledge of medicine which is generations ahead of anything known to Western science. And now, waste no more of my time. Listen—"

The big clock above the desk sounded its single note. Eight o'clock. The office door opened and Regan came in. His dour face wore an odd expression.

"I may be mistaken," he said, "but I fancy I saw a pair of tough-looking lads loafing outside the private door, downstairs."

Nayland Smith laughed. "Part of my bodyguard!"

"Oh," said Regan. "That's it, is it?"

"We are invested," murmured Craig. "A beleaguered garrison. Look well to your armour, gentlemen, and let your swords be bright."

Regan nodded unhumorously, and going up the steps, unlocked the laboratory door. Eerie vibrations invaded the office. His figure showed outlined for a moment against green light. Then the door was closed as he went in.

"I want to know," rapped Nayland Smith, "when you will be finished."

"Tonight."

"Sure?"

"Perfectly sure."

"I thought as much. Even allowing an hour for dinner?"

Craig brushed his hair back, staring.

"I'm stopping for no dinner."

Nayland Smith smiled again.

"Craig, I begin to agree with Dr. Fu Manchu, who informed me that you are what he described as 'touched with genius.' I don't want you to confirm his diagnosis by dying young. I have booked a table at a quiet restaurant. Until you are dragged away from that desk, your abstraction is deplorable. And there are many important things I want to tell you."

"Won't they keep?"

"No. And by the way, I miss the invaluable Sam."

"The said Invaluable has twenty-four hours' leave. His mother is ill in Philadelphia. Result, that for the first time in days I can go out for a drink without being tailed by a shadow in a peaked cap!"

"Oh!" rapped Smith, and gave Craig a steely glance. "Sorry to hear it."

The laboratory yawned again, and Shaw stepped out. He stood at the top of the steps for a moment, looking down. The chief technician had the heavy frame of an open-air man who has come indoors, a mass of unruly blond hair, and a merry eye.

"Just off, Shaw?" Craig called. "You don't know my masterful friend, Sir Denis Nayland Smith? On my right, Masterful Smith; on my left, Martin Shaw."

Shaw came down and shook hands.

"Free man until midnight," he said. "Then back to the bloody Juggernaut that lives in there!" He turned to Craig. "If you had that valve detail ready tonight, I believe I could fit up the transmuter in time for tests on, say, Monday."

"Do you?" Craig replied, and grinned like a schoolboy. "Has no thought crossed the massive brain to file a will before that date?"

Shaw nodded. "It has, Doctor. Rests with you. But if we can keep the cork in when we really fill the bottle, well—"

He went out, giving an imitation of a man under heavy fire. As the office door closed:

"Our convoy awaits!" said Nayland Smith. "Let's move."

"Stop ordering me about," Craig exclaimed in mock severity. "Oh, I give up the unequal contest."

He called the laboratory.

"Regan here."

"I regret to state, Regan, that I am being forcibly removed to some restaurant to dine—"

"Good thing, too."

"Repeat."

"I didn't say anything."

"Oh. Well, I shall be back at nine. Want to see me before I go?"

"No, Doctor. Enjoy your dinner."

Craig carried his drawing board, and his notes, across to the safe. When they were locked away, he glanced towards the door of Camille's room.

"She's out," said Smith drily. "I passed her as I came in."

They were already speeding along in a police car, two F.B.I. men following in another, when Camille faced Dr. Fu Manchu across the bizarre study.

"You have been here before," the harsh voice had said. And, in a moment of cold horror, which seemed to check her heartbeats, Camille knew this to be true. Her dream had haunted her so persistently that she had spoken to Morris, warned him to change the safe combination; for in her waste-basket she had found those fragments of a torn-up note. And although she had spent hours trying to piece the fragments together, and had failed, she knew that the paper on which the note was written came from the Huston Electric office.

Now—the man, the inscrutable, dreadful face of the man, every detail surrounding him, told her that the dream had been no dream, but a memory recaptured in sleep.

She had come to the appointment with Professor Hoffmeyer wearing her dark-rimmed glasses. At this moment the incongruity of her appearance in such an environment struck her forcibly.

One angle of the room was occupied by shelves filled with volumes, some of them large and in faded leather bindings. Then came the lacquer panel. This, she knew, masked an opening through which she had entered. Beyond it a curtain partly concealed a recess. There was an arched doorway in which a silk-shaded lantern hung.

A cushioned divan rose like an island in a sea of rugs. There were two strangely shaped mediaeval chairs.

A long black table bore books, open manuscripts, jars which apparently contained specimens of some kind, and a mummied head mounted on a wooden base. The dim light of a green lamp just outlined a crystal globe eclipsed in shadow.

And behind the table, hands with attenuated nails crossed under his chin, was the *Man* . . .

"Please sit down."

His half-closed eyes glanced sideways in the direction of the divan. He did not stir, otherwise.

Camille, fighting a desperate battle for calmness, for sanity, remained standing. She stared challengingly at the motionless figure. Her throat was dry, but when she spoke, her soft voice did not betray her.

"I came to consult Professor Hoffmeyer. Who are *you*?"

He remained immobile. When he replied, Camille could not see that the thin lips moved.

"I am accustomed to asking questions, Miss Navarre, not to answering them. But I must make a concession in the case of a fellow scientist — and one whose courage I respect. I am known as Dr. Fu Manchu."

"Dr. Fu Manchu!" she whispered.

"I believe you have been warned against me. I regret that, like the straying husbands, I should be so misunderstood, that the world should think badly of me."

"But what are you doing here? If Mrs. Frobisher knew—"

"If Mrs. Frobisher knew what? That Professor Hoffmeyer is Dr. Fu Manchu, or that Camille Navarre is employed by the intelligence service of an alien government? To which eventuality do you refer?"

"What do you say? What are you suggesting?"

"I suggest nothing. I ask a question. Mrs. Frobisher made the appointment for tonight because I told her to do so—"

"You mean—that Mrs. Frobisher knows—?"

"Mrs. Frobisher does not know anything. Few women do. But I believe that her husband might react unfavorably if he knew you to be an agent of Great Britain."

Camille's heart was throbbing wildly, but she had been trained to face the worst.

"Why do you say that?"

"Because it is true." Slowly Dr. Fu Manchu stood up. "Your employers are within their rights in seeking to learn the nature of those experiments being carried out in the Huston laboratory. We live in a dangerous age. I admire them for their ingenious removal to a better post of Dr. Craig's former assistant, and for providing you with the necessary credentials to take her place."

He was walking around the corner of the long, narrow table, and coming nearer. He had a catlike step.

"My credentials are my own."

140

"Indeed. And where did you acquire them?"

"Is that your business?"

Fear (the tall, yellow-robed figure was very close now) made her defiant.

"And where did you acquire them?" he repeated in a low, sibilant tone.

"I graduated at the Sorbonne."

"I congratulate you. These are details I had no time to gather at our former interview. And did you carry out intelligence work during the war?"

"I worked with the Resistance." Camille spoke faintly. "In Grenoble."

Dr. Fu Manchu returned to his seat behind the long table.

"Again, accept my congratulations. You speak perfect English."

"My mother was English."

Camille sank down on the divan. She was terrified, but her brain remained cool. One thing was clear. During that hiatus which had cost her so many sleepless nights, she must have been here. How had she got here? And why, except in a dream, had she completely forgotten all that happened?

Above all, what *had* happened? . . .

Camille clutched the cushions convulsively.

A quivering, metallic sound, like that of a distant sistrum, stirred the silence.

The crystal was coming to life. A radiance as of moonlight glowed and grew within it. For a moment it seemed cloudy, resembling a huge opal. Then the clouds dispersed, and a face materialized.

Camille thought, at first, that it was the living face of the Egyptian whose mummied head stood on the table, so yellow and wrinkled were its lineaments. But it soon declared itself as that of a very old Chinese.

"I have the report, Excellency."

The voice was clear, but seemed to come from a long way off.

"Repeat it."

Dr. Fu Manchu was watching the face in the crystal. A sudden urge to run flamed up in Camille's mind. She glanced swiftly right and left, and then:

"Remain where you are," came a harsh command. "There are no means of leaving this room without my permission. Continue, Huan Tsung."

"Nayland Smith and Dr. Craig are in the restaurant. Contact is impossible. There is an F.B.I. bodyguard at the doors. All my incoming messages are overheard. Therefore this was sent to me in the Shan dialect."

There came a momentary silence, in which Camille realized that she was not witnessing a supernatural phenomenon, but some hitherto unknown form of television; and then:

"I have one hour," said Dr. Fu Manchu, "in which to make the first move."

The face in the crystal faded slowly, like a mirage. The moonlight died away. As Dr. Fu Manchu turned his intolerable regard upon her again, Camille stood up.

"I want to know," she said, "why I have been trapped into coming here. Perhaps you think you can force me to betray Dr. Craig's secrets to you?"

"Were you not prepared to betray them to the British government?" he asked softly.

"Perhaps I was. But from a motive *you* could never

understand. In the hope of preserving the peace of the world—if that is possible."

"Do you regard Great Britain as holding a monopoly in peaceful intentions? Do you suppose that Dr. Craig would welcome the knowledge that you worked with him only to betray him?"

Camille tried to meet the gaze of those half-closed eyes. "I—I—did not think of it as betrayal. Only as a duty; a duty for which I must be prepared to sacrifice—everything."

"Such as the respect of Dr. Craig—or possibly something more precious?"

Camille lowered her eyes and dropped back on the divan. Dr. Fu Manchu stood up and walked towards her. He carried a small volume.

"I will never reveal one of Dr. Craig's secrets to you," she said on a note of desperation.

"My dear Miss Navarre—you have already revealed them all, or all that you knew at the time. Let you and me be sensible. Communist criminals aspire to rule man by fear. Nations no longer have the right to choose their rulers. As a result, the market is glutted with politicians, but statesmen are in short supply. Man wants nothing but happiness. What Russian yearns to spread the disease from which he himself is suffering?"

He stood right before her now.

"You see this book? It is a complete list of the megalomaniacs who are threatening the world with a third, and final, war. Power-drunk fools. They could all, quite easily, be assembled in this room. The unhappy peoples they claim to speak for are only the fuel to be thrown into the furnace of their mad lust.

Advance guards of these ignorant ruffians already knock at the door—and one man holds in his hands a weapon which may decide the issue."

"You mean—Dr. Craig?"

"I referred to him—yes."

Camille, with desperate courage, stood up and faced Fu Manchu.

"And you think I would put that weapon into *your* hands—even if I could? I should prefer to die—and leave the law to deal with *you!*"

But Dr. Fu Manchu remained unmoved.

"One who hopes to save civilization cannot afford to respect the law. You are that rare freak of the gods, a personable woman with a brain. Yet, womanlike, you permit emotion to rule you. Why do you wear those pieces of plain glass?"

He fully opened his strange eyes, raised one long-nailed hand, and pointed at her.

Camille ceased to possess any individual existence. She found herself in that trancelike condition which had made her dreams so terrible.

"Take them off."

Automatically she obeyed. Something within rose in fierce, angry revolt. But Camille herself was helpless.

"Shake your hair down."

She released her wonderful hair. It cascaded, a fiery torrent, onto her shoulders. Mechanically Camille arranged it with her fingers.

"Kneel."

She knelt at Fu Manchu's feet.

"Bow your head . . . Sleep."

She bowed her head, a beautiful, submissive slave

144

awaiting punishment.

Dr. Fu Manchu struck a silver bell which hung on a table beside the divan. Camille did not hear its sweet, lingering note. She was lost in a silent world from which only one sound could recall her—the voice of Fu Manchu.

A man entered through the archway. He never even glanced at the motionless, kneeling figure. He bowed, briefly but respectfully, to Fu Manchu. He was short, dark, and thickset, with a Teutonic skull. He wore a long, white-linen coat, like that of a surgeon.

Dr. Fu Manchu crossed and seated himself at the table.

"Koenig—tonight you will go to the Huston Building. The duplicate key you made after Miss Navarre's last visit opens the private door and also that of the elevator to the thirty-second floor. On the thirty-second floor there is another elevator. The key opens this also. Any questions?"

"No."

"It will take you to the thirty-sixth, where you will enter the office of Dr. Craig. The laboratory adjoins the office. The communicating door is locked. A man called Regan will be on duty in the laboratory. He must be induced to come out. Any questions?"

"No."

"M'goyna will be with you—if this alarms you, say so. Very well. Regan must be overpowered and taken back to the laboratory. M'goyna will then remain there with him. You will make it clear to Regan that should M'goyna be found there, he, Regan, will be

145

strangled. Regan must speak on intercommunication should Dr. Craig call him. Any questions?"

"No."

Dr. Fu Manchu clapped his hands sharply.

"M'goyna!"

The embroidered curtain which partly concealed a recess in the wall was drawn aside. A gigantic figure appeared. The shoulders of an Atlas, long arms, grotesquely large hands, and a face so scarred as to be incomparable with anything human. A red tarboosh crowned these dreadful features, and the figure wore white Arab dress, a scarlet sash, and Turkish slippers.

Slowly M'goyna came forward. Every movement was unnatural, like that of an automaton. The huge hands hung limp, insensate—the hands of a gorilla. Like a gorilla, too, he coughed hollowly as he entered.

Koenig clenched his fists, but stood still. Camille remained kneeling. M'goyna crossed to the long table and came to rest there facing Dr. Fu Manchu, who addressed him in Turkish.

"Change to street clothes. You go with Koenig to the Huston Building."

"With Koenig to the Huston Building," M'goyna intoned in a rasping voice.

"You will be shown a man. You must seize him."

"Shown a man. I seize him."

"You must not kill him."

M'goyna slowly revealed irregular, fanglike teeth and then closed his lips again. He coughed.

"Must not kill him."

"You are under Koenig's orders. Salute Koenig."

M'goyna touched his brow, his mouth, and his

breast and inclined his head.

"You will do as he tells you. At ten o'clock I shall come for you. Repeat the time."

"Ten o'clock—you come for me?"

"At ten o'clock." Dr. Fu Manchu turned to Koenig and spoke one word in English. "Proceed."

Morris Craig's office was empty. Night had dropped a velvet curtain outside the windows, irregularly embroidered with a black pattern where the darkened building opposite challenged a moonless sky.

Only the tubular desk lamp was alight, as Craig had left it.

So still was the place that when the elevator came up and stopped at the lobby, its nearly silent ascent made quite a disturbance. Then no movement was audible for fully a minute—when the office door opened inch by inch, and Koenig looked in. Satisfied with what he saw, he entered and crossed straight to Camille's room. This he inspected by the light of a flashlamp.

Noiseless in rubber soles, he moved to the laboratory door and shone a light onto the steps leading up to it. He examined the safe and went across to the long windows, staring out onto the terrace.

Then, turning his head, he spoke softly.

"M'goyna—"

M'goyna lumbered in. He wore brown overalls and a workman's cap. That huge frame, the undersized skull, were terrible portents. He stood just inside the door, motionless, a parody of humanity.

147

"Close the door."

M'goyna did so, and resumed his pose.

"The man will come out from there." Koenig pointed towards the laboratory. "Seize him."

M'goyna nodded his small head.

"Choke him enough but not too much—and then carry him back. You understand me?"

"Yes. Must not kill him."

"Hide here, between the couch and the steps. When he comes out, do as I have ordered. Remember—you must not kill him."

M'goyna nodded, and coughed.

"Are you ready?"

"Yes."

Koenig switched off the desk lamp. Now it was possible to see that the night curtain beyond the windows was studded with jewels twinkling in a cloudless heaven. Koenig shone the light of his lamp onto a recess between the leather-covered couch and the three steps.

"Here. Crouch down."

M'goyna walked across as if motivated by hidden levers and squatted there.

Koenig switched his lamp off. He paused for a moment to get accustomed to the darkness, then went up the three steps and beat upon the door with clenched fists.

"Regan!" he shouted. "Regan! . . . *Regan!* . . ."

He ran down and threw himself onto the couch beside which M'goyna waited.

Followed an interval of several seconds—ten—twenty—thirty.

Then came a faint sound. The steel door was

opened. Green light poured out, such a light as divers see below the surface of the ocean; rays giving no true illumination. The office became vibrant with unseen force.

Regan stood at the top of the steps, peering down. "Dr. Craig! Are you there?"

He began to descend, picking his way.

And, as his foot touched the bottom step, M'goyna hurled himself upon him, snarling like a wild animal.

"My God!"

The words were choked out of Regan. They faded into a gurgle, into nothing.

"Not too much! *Remember!*"

M'goyna grunted. One huge hand clasping Regan's throat, he lifted him with his free arm and carried him, like a bundle, up the steps.

Koenig followed.

The door remained open. Green light permeated the office filled with pulsations of invisible power. Then Koenig reappeared.

"You understand—he must answer calls. If Dr. Craig, or anyone else, comes in . . . you have your orders."

He closed the door behind him, so that silence, falling again, became a thing notable, almost audible. He stood still for a moment, taking his bearings, then crossed and switched up the desk lamp.

Noiselessly he went out.

The elevator descended.

chapter 12

"Wake!"

Camille opened her eyes, rose from her knees, and although her limbs felt heavy, cramped, sprang upright. She stared wildly at Dr. Fu Manchu, lifting one hand to her disarranged hair.

"What—what am I doing here?"

"You are kneeling to me as if I were the Buddha."

A wave of true terror swept over her. Almost, for the first time, she lost control.

"You . . . Oh, my God! What happened to me?"

She retreated from the tall, yellow-robed figure, back and back until her calves came in contact with the divan. Dr. Fu Manchu watched her.

"Compose yourself. Your chastity is safe with me. I wished to see you without your disguise."

"There was—someone else here—a dreadful man . . ."

"M'goyna? You were conscious of his presence? That is informative. I regret that I cannot give you an opportunity to examine M'goyna. As a fellow scientist, you would be interested. M'goyna carried my first invitation to you, although I thought you had forgotten."

"I had forgotten," Camille whispered. She was trembling.

"He can climb like an ape. He climbed from the fire ladders along the coping of the Huston Building in order to present my compliments. You spoke of 'a dreadful man.' But M'goyna is not a man. In Haiti he would be called a zombie. He illustrates the possibilities of vivisection. His frame is that of a Turkish criminal executed for strangling women. I recovered the body before rigor mortis had set in."

"You are trying to frighten me. Why?"

"Truth never frightened the scientific mind. M'goyna was created in my Cairo laboratory. I supplied him with an elementary brain — a trifle superior to that of a seal. Little more than a receiving set for my orders. He remains imperfect, however. I have been unable to rid my semihuman of that curious cough. Some day I must try again."

And, as the cold, supercilious voice continued, Camille began to regain her composure; for Dr. Fu Manchu had been unable wholly to conceal a note of triumph. He was a dangerous genius, probably a madman, but he was not immune from every human frailty . . . He was proud of his own fantastic achievements.

She dropped down onto the settee as he crossed, moving with that lithe, feline tread, and resumed his place behind the black table. When he spoke again he seemed to be thinking aloud . . .

"There are only a certain number of nature's secrets which man is permitted to learn. A number sufficient for his own destruction."

A high, wailing sound came from somewhere beyond the room. It rose, and fell, rose, and fell—and died away. But for Camille it was almost the last straw.

Clasping her hands, she sprang up, threatened now by hysteria.

"My God! What was it—"

Dr. Fu Manchu rested his chin on interlaced fingers.

"It was Bast—my pet cheetah. She thinks I have forgotten her supper. These hunting cats are so voracious."

"I don't believe you . . . It sounded like . . ."

"My dear Miss Navarre, I resent the implication. Sir Denis Nayland Smith would assure you that lying is not one of my vices."

Delicately he took a pinch of snuff from a silver box. Camille sat down again, struggling to recover her lost poise. She forced herself to meet his fixed regard.

"What is it you want? Why do you look at me like that?"

"I am admiring your beautiful courage. To destroy that which is beautiful is an evil thing." He stood up. "You wish for the peace of the world. You have said so. You fear cruelty. You flinched when you heard the cry of a cheetah. You have known cruelty—for there is no cruelty like the cruelty of war. If your wish was sincere, only *I* can hope to bring it true. Will you work *with* me, or *against* me?"

"How can I believe—"

"In Dr. Fu Manchu? In an international criminal? No—perhaps it is asking too much, in the time at my

152

disposal — and the very minutes grow precious." He opened his eyes widely. "Stand up, Camille Navarre. What is your real name?"

And Camille became swept again at command of the master hypnotist into that grey and dreadful half-world where there was no one but Dr. Fu Manchu.

"Camille Mirabeau," she answered mechanically — and stood up. "Navarre was the name by which I was known to the Maquis."

The green eyes were very close to hers.

"Why were you employed by Britain?"

"Because of my success in smuggling Air Force personnel out of the German zone. And because I speak several languages and have had science training."

"Were you ever married?"

"No."

"How many lovers have you had?"

"One."

"How long did this affair last?"

"For three months. Until he was killed by the Gestapo."

"Have you ceased to regret?"

"Yes."

"Does Morris Craig attract you?"

"Yes."

"He will be your next lover. You understand?"

"I understand."

"You will make him take you away from the Huston Building not later than half past nine. He must not return to his office tonight. You understand?"

"I understand."

"Does he find you attractive?"

"Yes."

The insistent voice was beating on her brain like a hammer. But she was powerless to check its beats, powerless to resist its promptings; compelled to answer—truthfully. Her brain, her heart, lay on Dr. Fu Manchu's merciless dissecting table.

"Has he expressed admiration?"

"Yes."

"In what way?"

"He has asked me not to wear glasses, and not to brush my hair back as I do."

"And you love him?"

Camille's proud spirit rose strong in revolt. She remained silent.

"You love him?"

It was useless. "Yes," she whispered.

"Tonight you will seduce him with your hair. The rest I shall leave to Morris Craig. I will give you your instructions before you leave. Sleep . . ."

There came an agonized interval, in which Camille lay helpless in invisible chains, and then the Voice again.

"I have forgotten all that happened since I left my office in the Huston Building. Repeat."

"I have forgotten all that happened since I left my office in the Huston Building."

"When I return I shall remember only what I have to do at nine-fifteen—nine-fifteen by the office clock."

"When I return I shall remember only what I have to do at nine-fifteen, by the office clock."

"At nine-thirty Dr. Fu Manchu will call me: repeat

154

the time."

"Nine-thirty."

"The fate of the world rests in my hands."

Camille raised her arms, clutching her head. She moaned . . . "Oh! . . . I . . . cannot bear this—"

"Repeat the words."

"The fate . . . of the world . . . rests . . . in . . . my hands . . ."

chapter 13

Morris Craig came back, "under convoy" from Nayland Smith's "quiet restaurant." Standing before the private door:

"Your restaurant was certainly quiet," he said. "But the check was a loud, sad cry. Come up if you like, Smith. But I have a demon night ahead of me. I *must* be through by tomorrow. Thanks for a truly edible dinner. Most acceptable to my British constitution. The wine was an answer to this pagan's prayer."

Nayland Smith gave him a long, steely-hard look.

"Have I succeeded in making it quite clear to you, Craig, that the danger is *now*, tonight, and for the next twenty-four hours?"

"Septically clear. Already I have symptoms of indigestion. But if I work on into the grey dawn I'm going to get the job finished, because I am bidden to spend the week-end with the big chief in the caves and jungles of Connecticut."

Nayland Smith, a lean figure in a well-worn tweed suit, for he had left his topcoat in the car, hesitated for a moment; then he grasped Craig firmly by the arm.

156

"I won't make myself a nuisance," he said. "But I want to see you right back on the job before I leave you. The fact is—I have a queer, uneasy feeling tonight. We must neglect no precaution."

And so they went up to the office together, and found it just as they had left it. Craig hung up hat and coat, grinning at Smith, who was lighting his pipe.

"Don't mind me. Carry on as if you were in your own abode. I'll carry on as if I were in mine."

He crossed to unlock the safe, when:

"Wait a minute," came sharply. "I'm going to make myself a nuisance after all."

Craig turned. "How come?"

"The duplicate key is in my topcoat! You will have to let me out."

"Blessings and peace," murmured Craig. "But I promise not to go beyond the street door. There will thus be no excuse for my being escorted upstairs again. Before we start, better let Regan know I'm back."

He called the laboratory, and waited.

"H'm. Silence. He surely can't have gone to sleep . . . Try him again."

And now came Regan's voice, oddly strained.

"Laboratory . . . Regan here."

"That's all right, Regan. Just wanted to say I'm back. Everything in order?"

"Yes . . . everything."

Craig glanced at Nayland Smith.

"Sounded very cross, didn't he?"

"Don't wonder. Is *he* expected to work all night, too?"

"No. Shaw relieves him at twelve o'clock."

"Come on then. I won't detain you any longer."

They went out.

That faint sound made by the elevator had just died away, when there came the muffled thud of two shots . . . The laboratory door was flung open—and Regan hurled himself down the steps. He held an automatic in his hand, as he raced towards the lobby.

"Dr. Craig! . . . Help! . . . *Dr. Craig!*"

Making a series of bounds incredible in a creature ordinarily so slow and clumsy of movement, M'goyna followed. His teeth were exposed like the fangs of a wild animal. He uttered a snarl of rage.

Regan twisted around and fired again.

Instant upon the crack of his shot, M'goyna dashed the weapon from Regan's grasp and swept him into a bear hug. Power of speech was crushed out of his body. He gave one gasping, despairing cry, and was silent. M'goyna lifted him onto a huge shoulder and carried him back up the steps.

Only a groan came from the laboratory when the semiman ran down again to recover Regan's pistol.

He coughed as he reclosed the steel door . . .

The office remained empty for another two minutes. Then Craig returned, swinging his keys on their chain. He went straight to the safe, paused—and stood sniffing. He had detected a faint but unaccountable smell. He glanced all about him, until suddenly the boyish smile replaced a puzzled frown.

"Smith's pipe!" he muttered.

Dismissing the matter lightly, as he always brushed aside—or tried to brush aside—anything which interfered with the job in hand, he had soon unlocked the safe and set up his materials. He was so deeply absorbed in his work that when Camille came in, he failed to notice even *her* presence.

She stood in the open doorway for a moment, staring vaguely about the office. Then she looked down at her handbag, and finally up at the clock above the desk. But not until she began to cross to her own room did Craig know she was there.

He spun around in a flash.

"Shades of evenin'! Don't play bogey man with me. My nerves are not what they were in my misspent youth."

Camille did not smile. She glanced at him and then, again, at the clock. She was not wearing her black-rimmed glasses, but her hair was tightly pinned back as usual. Craig wondered if something had disturbed her.

"I—I am sorry."

"Nothing to be sorry about. How's Professor What's-his-name? Full of beans and ballyhoo?"

"I—really don't know."

She moved away in the direction of her open door. Her manner was so strange that he could no longer ignore it. Insomnia, he knew, could play havoc with the nervous system. And Camille was behaving like one walking in her sleep. But when he spoke he retained the light note.

"What's the prescription—Palm Beach, or a round trip in the *Queen Elizabeth*?"

Camille paused, but didn't look back.

"I'm afraid—I have forgotten," she replied.

She went into her room.

Craig scratched his chin, looking at her closed

159

door. Certainly something was quite wrong. Could he have offended her? Was she laboring under a sense of grievance? Or was she really ill?

He took out a crushed packet of cigarettes from his hip pocket, smoothed one into roughly cylindrical form and lighted it; all the while staring at that closed door.

Very slowly, resuming his glasses, he returned to his work. But an image of Camille, wide-eyed, distrait, persistently intruded. He recalled that she had been in such a mood once before; and that he had made her go home. On the former occasion, too, she had been out but gave no account of where she had gone.

Something resembling a physical chill crept around his heart.

There was a man in her life. And he must have let her down . . .

Craig picked up a scribbling block and wrote a note in pencil. He was surprised, and angry, to find how shaky his hand had become. He must know the truth. But he would give her time. With a little tact, perhaps Camille could be induced to tell him.

He had never kissed her fingers, much less her lips, yet the thought of her in another man's arms drove him mad. He remembered that he had recently considered her place in the scheme of things, and had decided to dismiss such considerations until his work was completed.

Now he was almost afraid to press the button which would call her.

But he did.

He was back at his drawing board when he heard her come in. She moved so quietly that he sensed,

160

rather than knew, when she stood behind him. He tore off the top sheet and held it over his shoulder.

"Just type this out for me, d'you mind? It's a note for Regan. He can't read my writing."

"Of course, Dr. Craig."

Her soft voice soothed him, as always. How he loved it! He had just a peep of her delicate fingers as she took the page.

Then she was gone again.

Craig crushed out his cigarette in an ash-tray and sat staring at the complicated formula pinned to his drawing board. Of course, it probably meant something—something very important. It might even mean, as Nayland Smith seemed to think, a new era in the troubled history of man.

But why should he care *what* it meant if he must lose Camille?

He could hear her machine tapping . . .

Very soon, her door opened, and Camille came out. She carried a typed page and duplicates. The pencilled note was clipped to them. Craig didn't look up when she laid them beside the drawing board, and Camille turned to go. At the same moment, she glanced up at the clock.

Nine-fifteen . . .

Could Morris Craig have seen, he would have witnessed an eerie thing.

Camille's vacant expression became effaced; instantly, magically. She clenched her hands, fixing her eyes upward, upon the clock. For a moment she stood so, as if transfixed, as if listening intently. She symbolized vital awareness.

She relaxed, and, looking down, rested her left

161

hand on the desk beside Craig. She spoke slowly.

"I am sorry—if I have made any mistakes. Please tell me if this is correct."

Craig, who was not wearing his glasses, glanced over the typed page. He was trying desperately to think of some excuse to detain her.

"There was one word," the musical voice continued.

Camille raised her hands, and deliberately released her hair so that it swept down, a fiery, a molten torrent, brushing Craig's cheek as he pretended to read the message.

"Oh! Forgive me!"

She was bending over him when Craig twisted about and looked up into her eyes. Meeting his glance, she straightened and began to rearrange her hair.

He stood up.

"No—don't! Don't bother to do that."

He spoke breathlessly.

Camille, hands still lifted, paused, watching him. They were very close.

"But—"

"Your hair is—so wonderful." He clasped her wrists to restrain her. "It's a crime to hide it."

"I am glad you think so," she said rather tremulously.

He was holding her hands now. "Camille—would you think me a really fearful cad if I told you you are completely lovely?"

His heart seemed to falter when he saw that tiny curl of Camille's lip—like the stirring of a rose petal, he thought of it—heralding a smile. It was a new smile, a smile he had never seen before. She raised her lashes and looked into his eyes . . .

When he released her: "Camille," he whispered, "how *very* lovely you are!"

"Morris!"

He kissed her again.

"You darling! I suppose I have been waiting for this moment ever since you first walked into the office."

"Have you?"

This was a different woman he held in his arms—a woman who had disguised herself; this was the hidden, the secret Camille, seductive, wildly desirable—and his!

"Yes. Did you know?"

"Perhaps I did," she whispered.

Presently she disengaged herself and stood back, smiling provocatively.

"Camille—"

"Shall I take the message to Mr. Regan?"

Morris Craig inhaled deeply, and turned away. He was delirious with happiness, knew it, yet (such is the scientific mind) resented it. Camille had swept solid earth from beneath his feet. He was in the grip of a power which he couldn't analyze, a power not reducible to equations, inexpressible in a diagram. He had, perhaps, probed the secret of perpetual motion, exalting himself to a throne not far below the knees of the gods—but he had met a goddess in whose slender hands he was a thing of clay.

"D'you know," he said, glancing aside at her, "I think it might be a good idea if you did."

She detached the top copy of the note and walked

across to the laboratory steps.

"Will you open the door for me?"

Craig pulled out the bunch of keys and went to join her where she stood—one foot on the first step, her frock defining the lines of her slim body, reflected light touching rich waves of her hair to an incredible glory. Over her shoulder she watched him.

The keys rattled as he dropped the chain . . .

"Morris—please!"

He took the paper from her hand and tore it up. "Never mind. Work is out of the question, now."

"Oh, I'm so sorry!"

"You adorable little witch, you're not sorry at all! I thought I was a hard-boiled scientific egg until I met *you*."

"I'm afraid," said Camille demurely, and her soft voice reminded him again of the notes of a harp, "I have spoiled your plans for the evening."

"To the devil with plans! This is a night of nights. Let's follow it through."

He put his arm around her waist and dragged her from the steps.

"Very well, Morris. Whatever you say."

"I say we're young only once." He pulled her close. "At least, so far as we know. So I say let's be young together."

He gave her a kiss which lasted almost too long . . .

"Morris!"

"I could positively eat you alive!"

"But—your work—"

"Work is for slaves. Love is for free men. Where shall we go?"

"Anywhere you like, if you really mean it. But—"

"It doesn't matter. There are lots of spots. I feel that I want somewhere different, some place where I can get used to the idea that *you*—that there *is* a you, and that I have found you . . . I'm talkin' rot! Better let Regan know he's in sole charge again."

His keys still hung down on the chain as he had dropped them. He swung the bunch into his hand and crossed toward the steel door. At the foot of the steps, he hesitated. No need to go in. It would be difficult to prevent Regan from drawing inferences. Shrewd fellow, Regan. Craig returned to his desk and called the laboratory.

As if from far away a reply came:

"Regan here."

Craig cleared his throat guiltily.

"Listen, Regan. I shan't be staying late tonight after all." (He felt like a criminal.) "Pushing off. Anything I should attend to before Shaw comes on duty?"

There was a silent interval. Camille was standing behind Craig, clutching her head, staring at him in a dazed way . . .

"Can you hear, Regan? I say, do you want to see me before I leave?"

Then came the halting words. "No . . . Doctor . . . there's nothing . . . to see you about . . ."

Craig thought the sentence was punctured by a stifled cough.

A moment later he had Camille in his arms again.

"Camille—I realize that I have never been really alive before—"

But she was pressing her hands frantically against

165

him, straining back, wild-eyed, trying to break away from his caresses. He released her. She stared up at the clock—then back to Craig.

"My God! Morris! . . . Dr. Craig—"

"What is it, Camille? What is it?"

He stepped forward, but she shrank away.

"I don't know. I'm frightened. When—when did I come in? What have I been doing?"

His deep concern, the intense sincerity of his manner, seemed to reach her. When, gently, he held her and looked into her eyes, she lowered her head until it lay upon his shoulder, intoxicating him with the fragrance of her hair.

"Camille," he whispered, tenderly. (He could feel her heart beating.) "Tell me—what is it?"

"I don't know—I don't know what has happened. Please—please take care of me."

"Do you mean you have made a mistake? It was an impulse? You are sorry for it?"

"Sorry for what?" she murmured against his shoulder.

"For letting me make love to you."

"No—I'm not sorry if—if I did that."

He kissed her hair, very lightly, just brushing it with his lips.

"Darling! Whatever came over you? What frightened you?"

Camille looked up at him under her long lashes.

"I don't know." She lowered her eyes. "How long have I been here?"

"How long? What in heaven's name d'you mean, Camille? Are you terribly unhappy? I don't understand at all."

"No. I am not unhappy—but—everything is so strange."

"Strange? In what way?"

The phone rang in Camille's office. She started—stepped back, a sudden, alert look in her eyes.

"Don't trouble, Camille. I'll answer."

"No, no. It's quite all right."

Camille crossed to her room, and took up the phone. She knew it to be unavoidable that she should do this, but had no idea why. Some ten seconds later she had returned to the half-world controlled by the voice of Dr. Fu Manchu . . .

When she came out of her room again, she was smiling radiantly.

"It is the message I have waited for so long—to tell me that my mother, who is desperately ill, is no longer in danger."

Even as he took her in his arms, Craig was thinking that there seemed to be an epidemic of sick mothers, but he dismissed the thought as cynical and unworthy. And when she gave him her lips he forgot everything else. Her distrait manner was explained. The world was full of roses.

They were ready to set out before he fully came to his senses. Camille had combed her hair in a way which did justice to its beauty. She looked, as she was, an extremely attractive woman.

He stood in the lobby, his arm around her waist, preparing to open the elevator door, when sanity returned. Perhaps it was the sight of his keys which brought this about.

"By gad!" he exclaimed. "I *have* got it badly! Can you imagine—I was pushing off, and leaving the detail of the transmuter valve pinned to the board on my desk!"

He turned and ran back.

chapter 14

Somewhere in Chinatown a girl was singing.

Chinese vocalism is not everybody's box of candy, but the singer had at least one enthusiastic listener. She sang in an apartment adjoining the shop of Huan Tsung, and the good-looking shopman, who called himself Lao Tai, wrote at speed, in a kind of shorthand, all that she sang. From time to time he put a page of this writing into the little cupboard behind him and pressed a button.

The F.B.I. man on duty in a room across the street caught fragments of this wailing as they were carried to him on a slight breeze, and wondered how anyone who had ever heard Bing Crosby could endure such stuff.

But upstairs, in the quiet, silk-lined room, old Huan Tsung scanned page after page, destroying each one in the charcoal fire; and presently the globe beside his couch awoke to life, and the face of Dr. Fu Manchu challenged him from its mysterious depths.

"The latest report to hand, Excellency."

"Repeat it."

Huan Tsung leaned back against the cushions and

closed his wrinkled eyelids.

"I have installed the 'bazaar' system. My house is watched and my telephone is tapped. Therefore, news is brought to Mai Cha and she sings the news to Lao Tai."

"Spare me these details. The report."

"Reprimand noted. Dr. Craig and Camille Navarre left the Huston Building, according to Excellency's plan, at nine thirty-seven. One of the two detectives posted at the private entrance followed them. The other remains. No report yet to hand as to where Craig and the woman have gone."

"Nayland Smith?"

"Nothing later than former report. Raymond Harkness still acting as liaison officer in this area."

The widely opened green eyes were not focussed on Huan Tsung. A physician might have suspected the pinpoint pupils to indicate that Dr. Fu Manchu had been seeking inspiration in the black smoke. But presently he spoke, incisive, masterful as ever.

"Mount a diversion at four minutes to ten o'clock. Note the time. My entrance must be masked. Whoever is on duty—remove. But no assassinations. I may be there for an hour or more. Cover my retirement. My security is your charge. Proceed."

Light in the crystal died.

At a few minutes before ten o'clock, a man was standing at a bus stop twenty paces from the private entrance to the Huston laboratory. No bus that had pulled up there during the past hour had seemed to be the bus he was waiting for; and now he waited alone.

An uncanny quietude descends upon these office areas after dark. During the day they remind one of some vast anthill. Big-business ants, conscious of their fat dividends, neat little secretary ants, conscious of their slim ankles, run to and fro, in the restless, formless, meaningless dance of Manhattan.

Smart cabs and dowdy cabs, gay young cabs and sad old cabs, trucks, cars, busses, bicycles, pile themselves up in tidal waves behind that impassable barrier, the red light. And over in front of the suspended torrent scurry the big ants and the little ants. But at night, red and green lights become formalities. The ants have retired from the stage, but the lights shine on. Perhaps to guide phantom ants, shades of former Manhattan dancers now resting.

So that when a boy peddling a delivery bike came out of a street beside the Huston Building, it is possible that the driver of a covered truck proceeding at speed along the avenue failed to note the light.

However this may have been, he collided with the boy, who was hurled from his bicycle. The truckman pulled up with an ear-torturing screech of brakes. The boy—apparently unhurt—jumped to his feet and put up a barrage of abuse embellished with some of the most staggering invective which the man waiting for a bus had ever heard.

The truckman, a tough-looking bruiser, jumped from his seat, lifted the blasphemous but justly indignant youth by the collar of his jacket, and proceeded to punish him brutally.

This was too much for the man waiting for a bus. He ran to the rescue. The boy, now, was howling curses in a voice audible for several blocks. Spectators appeared — as they do — from nowhere. In a matter of seconds the rescuer, the rescued, and the attacker were hemmed in by an excited group.

And at just this moment, two figures alighted from the rear of the temporarily deserted truck, walked quietly to the private door of the Huston Building, opened it, and went in. Later, Raymond Harkness would have something to say to the man waiting for a bus — whose name was Detective Officer Beaker.

Huan Tsung had mounted a diversion . . .

The telephone in Camille's room was buzzing persistently — had been buzzing for a long time.

Craig had left the desk light burning; but most of the office lay in shadow, so that when someone switched on a flashlamp in the lobby, a widening, fading blade of light swept across the parquet floor. Then the door was fully opened.

Koenig stepped in, looking cautiously about him. He carried a heavy leather case, which he set down by the safe.

And, as he stood upright again, a tall figure, draped in a black topcoat, the fur collar turned up, came in silently and joined him. Dr. Fu Manchu wore the tinted Hoffmeyer glasses, gloves, and carried a black hat. He looked in the direction of that persistent buzzing.

"Miss Navarre's office," said Koenig uneasily.

Dr. Fu Manchu indicated the safe, merely extending a gloved hand. Koenig nodded, knelt, and opened the leather case. Taking out a bunch of keys, he busied himself with the lock, working by the light of his flashlamp. Presently he paused. He turned.

"Combination has been changed!"

The tall figure standing behind him remained motionless. The buzzing in Camille's room ceased.

"You came prepared for such a possibility?"

"Yes—but it may take a long time now."

"You have nearly two hours. But no more."

The clock over Craig's desk struck its single note . . . ten o'clock.

Dr. Fu Manchu crossed and walked up the three steps. He beat upon the steel door.

"M'goyna!"

The door swung open. M'goyna's huge frame showed silhouetted against a quivering green background.

Dr. Fu Manchu entered the laboratory.

At half-past eleven, the man waiting for a bus was relieved by another detective. The avenue, now, was as completely deserted as any Manhattan avenue ever can be.

"Hello, Holland," he said. "You're welcome to this job! Like being the doorman of a vacant night club."

"What are we supposed to be doing, Beaker, anyway?"

"Search me! Stop anybody going in, I suppose. We had orders to tail Dr. Craig if ever *he* came out, and Stoddart went after him two hours ago when he took his secretary off to make whoopee. A redhead straight from heaven."

"Nothing else happened?"

"Bit of a scrap about ten o'clock. Big heel driving a truck knocked a boy off his bike. Nothing else . . . Goodnight."

"Goodnight."

Holland lighted a cigarette, looking left and right along the avenue and wondering what had originally attracted him to police work. Beaker was making for a subway station and Holland followed the retreating figure with his eyes for several blocks. He settled down to a monotony broken only by an occasional bus halting at the nearby stop. The night was unseasonably warm.

At a quarter to twelve, a remarkable incident occurred.

It had been preceded by another curious occurrence, invisible to Holland, however. A red light had been flashed several times from the high parapet of the Huston Building, immediately outside Craig's office . . .

Bearing down upon Holland at speed from the other end of the block, he saw a hatless young man in evening dress, who *screamed* as he ran!

"You won't get me! You devils! You won't get me!"

In spite of the emptiness of the streets, these outcries had had some effect. Two men were following, but maintaining a discreet distance from the screaming man. Keeping up that extraordinary pace, he drew nearer and nearer to Holland.

"Out of my way! They're after me!"

Holland sized up the situation. The runner was of medium build, dark, and not bad-looking in a Latin fashion. Clearly, Holland decided, he's drunk, and a guy in that state is doubly strong. But I guess I'll have to hold him. He may do damage.

An experienced manhandler, Holland stepped forward. But the runner kept on running.

"Out of my way!" he screamed. "I'll kill you if you try to stop me!"

Holland stooped for a tackle, saw the gleam of a weapon, and side-stepped in a flash.

"They won't get me!" yelled the demented man, and went racing around the corner.

Had the missing Sam been present, he would have recognized the lunatic as that Jed Laurillard who had once talked to him in a bar. In fact, this disciple had been given a particularly difficult assignment, one certain to land him in jail, as a chance to redeem his former mistake. He had, furthermore, been given a shot of hashish to lend color to the performance.

Holland clapped a whistle to his lips, and blew a shrill blast. Drawing his own automatic, he went tearing around the corner after the still screaming madman . . .

During a general mix-up which took place there, a big sedan drew in before the private door of the Huston Building, and three men came out and entered it. One of them carried a heavy roll of office carpet on his shoulder.

Huan Tsung had successfully covered the retirement of Dr. Fu Manchu.

When Martin Shaw stepped from a taxi, paid the driver, and saw the yellow cab driven away, he unbuttoned his topcoat to find his key. Someone was walking rapidly towards him; the only figure in sight. It was midnight.

Holland, whilst still some distance away, recognized the chief technician, and moderated his pace.

The screaming alcoholic had just been removed in charge of two patrolmen, and would, no doubt, receive his appropriate medicine in the morning. By the time Holland reached the door, Shaw had already gone in, and was on his way up.

Shaw half expected that Dr. Craig would be still at work, and even when he didn't see him at his desk, was prepared to find him in the laboratory. Then he noted that the drawing board was missing and the safe locked. Evidently, Craig had gone.

Whoever took the next (four-to-eight) duty usually slept on a couch in the office. But Regan seemed to have made no preparations.

Shaw went up the three steps and unlocked the steel door.

"Here we are, Regan!" he called in his breezy way. "Get to hell out of it, man!"

There was no reply. Everything seemed to be in order. But where was Regan?

Then, pinned to the logbook lying on a glass-topped table, Shaw saw a sheet of ruled paper. He crossed and bent over it.

A message, written shakily in Regan's hand, appeared there. It said:

Mr. Shaw—
Had a slight accident. Compelled to go for medical treatment. Don't be alarmed. Will report at 4 A.M. for duty.

J. J. Regan

"Slight accident?" Shaw muttered.

He looked keenly about him. What could have

happened? There was nothing wrong with any of the experimental plant. He quickly satisfied himself on that score. So unlike Regan not to have timed the message. He wondered how long he had been gone. The last entry in the log (almost illegible) was timed eleven-fifteen.

He was hanging his coat up when he noticed the bloodstains.

They were very few—specks on white woodwork. But, stooping, he came to the conclusion that others had been wiped from the tiled floor below.

Regan, then, must have cut himself in some way, been unable to staunch the bleeding, and gone to find a surgeon. Shaw decided that he had better notify Dr. Craig. The laboratory phone was an extension from the secretary's office. He reopened the door, went down the steps, and dialled from Camille's room.

There was no answer to his call.

Shaw growled, but accepted the fact philosophically. He would repeat the call later. He went back to his working-bench in the laboratory and was soon absorbed in adjusting an intricate piece of mechanism in course of construction there. He walked in an atmosphere vibrant with a force new to science. His large hands were delicate as those of a violinist . . .

He called Craig's number again at one o'clock, but there was no reply. He tried Regan's, with a similar result. Perhaps the injury was more serious than Regan had supposed. He might have been detained for hospital treatment.

Shaw tried both numbers again at two and then at three o'clock. No answers.

He began to feel seriously worried about Regan;

nor could he entirely understand the absence of Craig. He knew how determined Craig had been to complete the valve detail that night, he knew he was spending the week-end away; and he felt sure that Morris Craig wasn't the man to waste precious hours in night spots.

In this, Shaw misjudged Craig—for once. At almost exactly three o'clock, that is, whilst Shaw was vainly calling his number, Morris Craig leaned on a small table, feasting his eyes on Camille, who sat facing him.

"Say you are happy," he whispered.

That *she* was happy, that this new wonderland was real and not a mirage, seemed to him, at the moment, the only thing that mattered—the one possible excuse for his otherwise inexcusable behavior.

Camille smiled, and then lowered her eyes. She knew that she had been dancing—dancing for hours, it seemed to her. Even now, a band played softly, somewhere on the other side of a discreetly dim floor. Yes—she was happy. She was in love with Morris, and they were together. But how could she surrender herself to all that such an evening should mean, when she had no idea how she came to be there?

She knew that she had set out to keep an appointment made for her by Mrs. Frobisher. Had she kept it? Apart from a vague recollection of talking to Morris in the office—of some sudden terror—the rest of the night remained a blank up to the moment when she had found herself here, in his arms, dancing.

"Yes—I am happy, Morris, very happy. But I think I must go home now."

It was nearly half past three when they left.

In the little lobby of her apartment house, between swing doors and the house door, Craig held her so long that she thought he would never let her go. Every time she went to put her key in the lock, he pulled her back and held her again. At last:

"I shall be here for you at nine in the morning," he said.

"All right. Good night, Morris."

She opened the door, and was gone. He watched her, through glass panels, as she hurried upstairs. Then he went out, crossed the street, and waited to see a light spring up in her room. When one did, he still waited — and waited.

At last she came to the window, pulled a drape aside, and waved him good night.

He had dismissed the taxi. He wanted to walk, to be alone with this night, to relive every hour of the wonder that had come into his life with Camille's first kiss.

When, at Central Park West, he decided to walk across the Park, two tired and bored detectives who had been keeping the pair in sight ever since they had left the night club, exhaled self-pitying sighs . . .

chapter 15

At ten past four, Martin Shaw dialled Regan's number. No reply. Then he tried Craig's. No reply. Following a momentary hesitation, he called police headquarters.

He had no more than begun to explain what had happened when he heard the clang of the elevator door as someone slammed it shut. Laying the phone down on Camille's desk, he ran out into Craig's office. He arrived just as Nayland Smith burst in.

"Sir Denis! What's this?"

Nayland Smith was darting urgent glances right and left.

"Where's Regan?" he rapped.

"Hasn't shown up—"

"What!"

"Had an accident some time before I returned. Left a note."

Nayland Smith's challenging stare was almost frightening.

"You mean the place was *empty* when you arrived at twelve?"

"Just that."

"And you did nothing about it?"

"Why should I?" Shaw demanded. "But when he didn't appear at four o'clock, it was different. I have police headquarters on the line right now—"

"Tell them I'm here. Then hang up."

Shaw, upon whom this visitor had swept as a typhoon, went back and did so.

"I know," a voice replied. "We're on the job. Stand by."

When Shaw rejoined him:

"Your handyman, Sam, was got away by a ruse," said Smith. "He wisely called the police, too—from Philadelphia. I came straight along. Someone wanted this place vacated tonight—and Craig played right into the enemy's hands—"

"But where *is* the Doctor? I have been calling him—"

"You'd be surprised!" Smith snapped savagely. "At the present moment, he's wandering around Central Park, moonstruck! One of two men looking after him got to a phone ten minutes ago."

Shaw looked thunderstruck.

"Has he gone mad?"

"Yes. He's in love. Show me this note left by Regan."

He went racing up the steps. Shaw had left the laboratory door open.

"There—on the table."

Nayland Smith bent over Regan's strange message. He turned.

"Sure it's his writing?"

"Looks like it—allowing for a shaky hand. He'd evidently cut himself. See—there are specks of blood here." Shaw pointed. "And I think blood has been wiped from the floor just below."

Nayland Smith pulled at the lobe of his ear. His brown face looked drawn, weary, but his eyes shone like steel. The green twilight of this place, the eerie throbbing which seemed to penetrate his frame, he disliked, but knew he must ignore. A moment he stood so, then turned and ran back to the phone. He called police headquarters, gave particulars of what had happened, and:

"Check all night taxis," he directed rapidly, "operating in this area. All clinics and hospitals in the neighborhood. Recall Detectives Beaker and Holland, on duty at the door here between eight and four. Order them to report to Raymond Harkness."

He hung up, called another number, and presently got Harkness.

"I'm afraid we lose, Harkness," he said. "I'm at the Huston Building. Something very serious has occurred tonight. I fear the worst. The two men posted below must have tripped up, somewhere. They will report to you. Make each take oath and swear he never left the door for a moment. Then call me. I shall be here. . . ."

In the throbbing laboratory, Martin Shaw was making entries in the log. He looked up as Nayland Smith came in.

"Of course," he said, "I can see something has happened to poor Regan. But it's not clear to me that there's anything else to it."

"Not clear?" rapped Smith. "Why should a man who generally hangs around the place at all hours — Sam — receive a faked call to get him to Philadelphia?

182

Is it a mere coincidence that Regan deserts his post the same night? For some time before twelve o'clock—we don't know for how long—no one was on duty here."

"There's an entry in the book timed eleven-fifteen."

"Very shaky one. Still leaving a gap of forty-five minutes."

"If you mean some foreign agent got in, *how* did he get in?"

"He probably had a duplicate key, as I have. The F.B.I. got mine from the locksmith who made the originals. Couldn't someone else have done the same thing? Or borrowed, and copied, an existing key?"

"But nothing has been disturbed. There's no evidence that anyone has been here."

"There wouldn't be!" said Smith grimly. "Dangerous criminals leave no clues. The visitor I suspect would only want a short time to examine the plant—and to borrow Craig's figure of the transmuter valve—"

"That would mean opening the safe."

"Exactly what *we* have to do—open the safe."

"No one but Dr. Craig has a key—or knows the combination."

"There are other methods," said Nayland Smith drily. "I am now going out to examine the safe."

He proceeded to do so, and made a thorough job of it. Shaw came down and joined him.

"Nothing to show it's been tampered with," Smith muttered . . . "Hullo! who comes?"

He had detected that faint sound made by the private elevator. He turned to face the lobby; so did Shaw.

183

The elevator ascended, stopped. A door banged. And Morris Craig ran in.

"Smith!" he exclaimed—and both men saw that he was deathly pale. "What's this? What has happened? I was brought here by two detectives—"

"Serves you right!" rapped Nayland Smith. "Don't talk. Act. Be good enough to open this safe."

"But—"

"Open it."

Craig, his hand none too steady, pulled out his keys, twirled the dial, and opened the safe. Nayland Smith and Martin Shaw bent over his shoulders.

They saw a number of papers, and Craig's large drawing board.

But there was nothing on the board!

A moment of silence followed—ominous silence. Then Nayland Smith faced Craig.

"I don't know," he said, and spoke with unusual deliberation, "what lunacy led you to desert your job tonight. But I am anxious to learn"—he pointed— "what has become of the vital drawing and the notes, upon which you were working."

Morris Craig forced a smile. It was an elder brother of the one he usually employed. Some vast, inexpressible relief apparently had brought peace to his troubled mind.

"If that's all," he replied, "the answer's easy. I had a horrible idea that—something had happened—to Camille."

Nayland Smith exchanged a glance with Shaw.

"Ignoring the Venusburg music for a moment"—

the words were rapped out in his usual staccato manner—"where is the diagram?"

Morris Craig smiled again—and the junior smile was back on duty. He removed his topcoat, stripped his jacket off, and groped up under his shirt. From this cache he produced a large, folded sheet of paper and another, smaller sheet—the one decorated with a formula like a Picasso painting.

"In spite of admittedly high temperature at time of departure, I remembered that I was leaving town in the morning. I decided to take the job with me. If"—he glanced from face to face—"you suspect some attempt on the safe, all the burglar found was—Old Mother Hubbard. I carry peace to Falling Waters."

chapter 16

The library at Falling Waters was a pleasant room. It was panelled in English oak imported by Stella Frobisher. An open staircase led up to a landing which led, in turn, to rooms beyond. There were recessed bookcases. French windows gave upon a paved terrace overlooking an Italian garden. Sets of Dickens, Thackeray, *Punch*, and *Country Life* bulked large on the shelves.

There was a handsome walnut desk, upon which a telephone stood, backed by a screen of stamped Spanish leather. Leather-covered armchairs and settees invited meditation. The eye was attracted (or repelled) by fine old sporting prints. Good Chinese rugs were spread on a well-waxed floor.

Conspicuous above a bookcase, and so unlike Stella's taste, one saw a large glazed cabinet containing a colored plan of the grounds surrounding Falling Waters. It seemed so out of place.

On occasional tables, new novels invited dipping. Silver caskets and jade caskets and cloisonné caskets contained cigarettes to suit every palate. There were discreet ornaments. A good reproduction of Queen

Nefertiti's beautiful, commercialized head above a set of Balzac, in French, which no member of this household could read. A bust of Shakespeare. A copy of the Discus Thrower apparently engaged in throwing his discus at a bust by Epstein on the other side of the library.

A pleasant room, as sunshine poured in to bring its lifeless beauties to life, to regild rich bindings, on this morning following those strange occurrences in the Huston research laboratory.

Michael Frobisher was seated at the walnut desk, the phone to his ear. Stein, his butler-chauffeur, stood at his elbow. Michael Frobisher was never wholly at ease in his own home. He remained acutely conscious of the culture with which Stella had surrounded him. This morning, his unrest was pathetic.

"But this thing's just incredible! . . . What d'you say? You're certain of your facts, Craig? Regan never left a note like that before? . . . What d'you mean, he hasn't come back? He must be in some clinic . . . The police say he isn't? To hell with the police! I don't want police in the Huston laboratory . . . You did a wise thing there, but I guess it was an accident . . . Bring the notes and drawing right down here. For God's sake, bring 'em right down here! How do we know somebody hasn't explored the plant? Listen! how do we know?"

He himself listened awhile, and then:

"To hell with Nayland Smith!" he growled. "Huston Electric doesn't spend half a million dollars to tip the beans into *his* pocket. He's a British agent. He'll sell us out! Are you crazy? . . . He *may* be backed by Washington. What's good that comes to us from

Washington, anyway?"

He listened again, and suddenly:

"Had it occurred to you," he asked on a note of tension, "that *Regan* could be the British agent? He joined us from Vickers . . ."

When at last he hung up:

"Is there anything you want me to do?" Stein asked.

Stein was a man who, seated, would have looked like a big man, for he had a thick neck, deep chest, and powerful shoulders. But, standing, he resembled Gog, or Magog, guardian deities of London's Guildhall; a heavy, squat figure, with heavy, squat features. Stein wore his reddish hair cut close as a Prussian officer's. He had a crushed appearance, as though someone had sat on his head.

Frobisher spun around. "Did you get it?"

"Yes. It is serious." (Stein furthermore had a heavy, squat accent.) "But not so serious as if they have found the detail of the transmuter."

"What are you talking about?" Frobisher stood up. "There's enough in the lab to give away the whole principle to an expert."

That grey undertone beneath his florid coloring was marked.

"This may be true—"

"And Regan's disappeared!"

"I gathered so."

"Then—hell!"

"You are too soon alarmed," said Stein coolly. "Let us wait until we have all the facts."

"How'll we *ever* have all the facts?" Frobisher demanded. "What are the facts about things that happen right here? Who walks around this house at night like a ghost? Who combed my desk papers? Who opened my safe? And who out of hell went through *your* room the other evening while you were asleep? Tell me *who*, and then tell me *why!*"

But before Stein had time to answer these reasonable inquiries, Stella Frobisher fluttered into the library. She wore a Hollywood pinafore over her frock, her hands were buried in gauntlet gloves, and she carried a pair of large scissors. Her blond hair was dressed as immaculately as that of a movie star just rescued from a sinking ship.

"I *know* I look a *fright*, dear," she assured Frobisher. "I have been out in the garden, *cutting* early spring flowers."

She emphasized "cutting" as if her more usual method was to knock their heads off with a niblick.

"Allow me to bring these in for you, madame," said Stein.

His respectful manner was in odd contrast to that with which he addressed Frobisher.

"Thank you, Stein. Lucille has the *basket* on the *back* porch."

She did not mention the fact that Lucille had also cut the flowers.

"Very good, madame."

As Stein walked towards the door:

"Oh, Stein—there will be *seven* to luncheon. Dr. and *Mrs.* Pardoe are coming."

Stein bowed and went out.

"Who's the odd man?" growled Frobisher, opening a box of cigars which lay on the desk.

"Professor Hoffmeyer. Isn't it *splendid* that I got

him to come?"

"Don't know till I see him."

"He's simply *wonderful*. He will *amaze* you, Mike."

"Don't care for amazement at mealtimes."

"You will fall *completely* under his *spell*, dear," Stella declared, and went fluttering out again. "I must go and *assemble* my flowers."

At about this time, Morris Craig was putting a suitcase into the back of his car. As he locked the boot he looked up.

"You know, Smith," he said, "I'm profoundly conscious of the gravity of this thing—but I begin to feel like a ticket-of-leave man. There's a car packed with police on the other side of the street. Do they track me to Falling Waters?"

"They do!" Nayland Smith replied. "As I understand it, you are now going to pick up Miss Navarre?"

"That is the program." Craig smiled rather unhappily. "I feel a bit cheap leaving Shaw alone, in the circumstances. But—"

"Shaw won't be alone!" Smith rapped irritably. "I think—or, rather, fear—the danger at the laboratory is past. But, to make sure, two carefully selected men will be on duty in your office day and night until you return. Plus two outside."

"Why not Sam? He's back."

"You will need Sam to lend a hand with this radio burglar alarm you tell me about—"

"*I* shall?"

"You will. I can see you're dying to push off. So—push! I trust you have a happy week-end."

And when Craig turned into West Seventy-fifth

Street, the first thing that really claimed his attention was the presence of a car which had followed him all the way. The second was a figure standing before the door of an apartment house—a door he could never forget.

This figure wore spectacles, a light fawn topcoat, a cerise muffler, and a slate-grey hat with the brim turned up not at the back, but in front . . .

"Morning, boss," said Sam, opening the door. "Happen to have—"

"I have nothing but a stern demand. It's this: What the devil are you doing *here*?"

"Well"—Sam shook his head solemnly—"it's like this. Seems you're carrying valuables, and Sir Denis, he thinks—"

"He thinks what?"

"He thinks somebody ought to come along—see? Just in case."

Craig stepped out.

"Tell me: Are you employed by Huston Electric or by Nayland Smith?"

Sam tipped his hat further back. He chewed thoughtfully.

"It's kind of complicated, Doctor. Sir Denis has it figured I'm doing my best for Huston's if I come along and lend a hand. He figures there may be trouble up there. And you never know."

Visions of a morning drive alone with Camille vanished.

"All right," said Craig resignedly. "Sit at the back."

In a very short time he had hurried in. But it was a long time before he came out.

Camille looked flushed, but delightfully pretty, when she arrived at Falling Waters. Her hair was tastefully dressed, and she carried the black-rimmed glasses in her hand. Stella was there to greet her guests.

"My *dear* Miss Navarre! It's so *nice* to have you *here* at last! Dr. Craig, you have kept her in *hiding* too long."

"Not my fault, Mrs. Frobisher. She's a self-effacing type." Then, as Frobisher appeared: "Hail, chief! Grim work at —"

Frobisher pointed covertly to Stella, making vigorous negative signs with his head. "Glad to see you, Craig," he rumbled, shaking hands with both arrivals.

"You have a charming house, Mrs. Frobisher," said Camille. "It was sweet of you to ask me to come."

"I'm so *glad* you like it!" Stella replied. "Because you must have seen such *lovely* homes in France and in England."

"Yes," Camille smiled sadly. "Some of them *were* lovely."

"But let me take you along to your *room*. This is your *first* visit, but I do *hope* it will be the first of *many*."

She led Camille away, leaving Frobisher and Craig standing in the lobby — panelled in Spanish mahogany from the old Cunard liner, *Mauretania*. And at that moment Frobisher's eye rested upon Sam, engaged in taking Craig's suitcase from the boot, whilst Stein stood by.

"What's that half-wit doing down here?" Frobisher

inquired politely.

"D'you mean Sam? Oh, he's going to — er — lend me a hand overhauling your burglar system."

"Probably make a good job of it, between you," Frobisher commented drily. "When you've combed your hair, Craig, come along to my study. We have a lot to talk about. Where's the plan?"

Craig tapped his chest. He was in a mood of high exaltation.

"On our person, good sir. Only over our dead body could caitiffs win to the treasure."

And in a room all daintily chintz, with delicate water colors and lots of daffodils, Camille was looking out of an opened window, at an old English garden, and wondering if her happiness could last.

Stein tapped at the door, placed Camille's bag inside, and retired.

"Don't *bother* to unpack, my dear," said Stella. "Flora, my maid, is *superlative.*"

Camille turned to her, impulsively.

"You are very kind, Mrs. Frobisher. And it was so good of you to make that appointment for me with Professor Hoffmeyer."

"With Professor Hoffmeyer? Oh! my dear! *Did* I, really? Of course" — seeing Camille's strange expression — "I *must* have done. It's queer and it's *absurd,* but, do you know, I'm *addicted* to the oddest *lapses* of memory."

"*You* are?" Camille exclaimed; then, as it sounded so rude, she added, "I mean *I* am, too."

"*You* are?" Stella exclaimed in turn, and seized both her hands. "Oh, my dear, I'm *so* glad! I mean, I know I *sound* silly, and a bit *horrid*. What I *wanted* to say was, it's such a *relief* to meet somebody *else* who suffers in that *way*. Someone who has no possible *reason* for going funny in the head. But *tell* me—what did you *think* of him?"

Camille looked earnestly into the childish but kindly eyes.

"I must tell you, Mrs. Frobisher—impossible though it sounds—that I have no recollection whatever of going there!"

"My dear!" Stella squeezed her hands encouragingly. "I *quite* understand. Whatever do you *suppose* is the matter with us?"

"I'm afraid I can't even imagine."

"*Could* it be some new kind of *epidemic*?"

Camille's heart was beating rapidly, her expression was introspective; for she was, as Dr. Fu Manchu had told her (but she had forgotten), a personable woman with a brain.

"I don't know. Suppose we compare notes—"

Michael Frobisher's study, the window of which offered a prospect of such woodland as Fenimore Cooper wrote about, was eminently that of a man of business. The books were reference books, the desk had nothing on it but a phone, a blotting-pad, pen, ink, a lamp, an almanac, and a photograph of Stella. The safe was built into the wall. No unnecessary litter.

"There's the safe I told you about," he was saying. "There's the key—and the combination is right here." He touched his rugged forehead. "Yet—I found the damned thing wide open! My papers"—he pulled out a drawer—"were sorted like a teller sorts checks. *I* know. I always have my papers in order. Then—

194

somebody goes through my butler's room." He banged his big fist on the desk. "And not a bolt drawn, not a window opened!"

"Passing strange," Craig murmured. He glanced at the folded diagram. "Hardly seems worth while to lock it up."

Michael Frobisher stared at the end of his half-smoked cigar, twirling it between strong fingers.

"There's been nothing since I installed the alarm system. But I don't trust anybody. I want you to test it. Meanwhile" — he laid his hand on the paper — "how long will it take you to finish this thing?"

"Speaking optimistically, two hours."

"You mean, in two hours it will be possible to say we're finished?"

"Hardly. Shaw has to make the valves. Wonderful fellow, Shaw. Then we have to test the brute in action. When that bright day dawns, it may be the right time to say we're finished!"

Frobisher put his cigar back in his hard mouth, and stared at Craig.

"You're a funny guy," he said. "It took a man like me to know you had the brains of an Einstein. I might have regretted the investment if Martin Shaw hadn't backed you — and Regan. I'm doubtful of Regan — now. But he knows the game. Then — you've shown me things."

"A privilege, Mr. Frobisher."

Frobisher stood up.

"Don't go all Oxford on me. Listen. When this detail here is finished, you say we shall be in a position to tap a source of inexhaustible energy which completely tops atomic power?"

"I say so firmly. Whether we can control the monster depends entirely upon—that."

"The transmuter valve?"

"Exactly. It's only a small gadget. Shaw could make all three of 'em in a few hours. But if it works, Mr. Frobisher, and I *know* it will, we shall have at our command a force, cheaply obtained, which could (a) blow our world to bits, or (b) enable us to dispense with costly things like coal, oil, enormous atomic plants, and the like, forever. I am beginning to see tremendous possibilities."

"Fine."

Michael Frobisher was staring out of the window. His heavy face was transfigured. He, too, the man of commerce, the opportunist, could see those tremendous possibilities. No doubt he saw possibilities which had never crossed the purely scientific mind of Morris Craig.

"So," said Craig, picking up the diagram and the notes, "I propose that I retire to my cubicle and busy myself until cocktails are served. Agreed?"

"Agreed. Remember—not a word to Mrs. F."

When Craig left the study, Frobisher stood there for a long time, staring out of the window.

But Morris Craig's route to his "cubicle" had been beset by an obstacle—Mrs. F. As he crossed the library towards the stair, she came in by another door. She glanced at the folded diagram.

"My *dear* Dr. Craig! Surely you haven't come *here* to work?"

Craig pulled up, and smiled. Stella had always liked

his smile; it was so English.

"Afraid, yes. But not for too long, I hope. If you'll excuse me, I'll nip up and get going right away."

"But it's too *bad*. How soon will you be *ready* to nip *down* again?"

"Just give me the tip when the bar opens."

"Of *course* I will. But, you know, I have been *talking* to Camille. She is *truly* a dear girl. I *don't* mean expensive. I *mean* charming."

Craig's attention was claimed, magically, by his hostess's words.

"So glad you think so. She certainly is—brilliant."

Stella Frobisher smiled her hereditary smile. She was quite without sex malice, and she had discovered a close link to bind her to Camille.

"Why don't you *forget* work? Why don't you two *scientific* people go for a walk in the *sunshine?* After all, that's what you're *here* for."

And Morris Craig was sorely tempted. Yes, that was what he was here for. But—

"You see, Mrs. Frobisher," he said, "I rather jibbed the toil last night. Camille—er—Miss Navarre, has been working like a pack-mule for weeks past. Tends to neglect her fodder. So I asked her to step out for a plate of diet and a bottle of vintage—"

"That was *so* like you, Dr. Craig."

"Yes—I'm like that. We sort of banished dull care for an hour or two, and as a matter of fact, carried on pretty late. The chief is anxious about the job. He has more or less given me a deadline. I'm only making up for lost time. And so, please excuse me. Sound the trumpets, beat the drum when cocktails are served."

He grinned boyishly and went upstairs. Stella went to look for Camille. She had discovered, in this young product of the Old World, something that the New World had been unable to give her. Stella Frobisher was often desperately lonely. She had never loved her husband passionately. Passion had passed her by.

In the study, Michael Frobisher had been talking on the phone. He had just hung up when Stein came in.

"Listen," he said. "What's this man, Sam, doing here?"

Stein's heavy features registered nothing.

"I don't know."

"Talk to him. Find out. I trust nobody. *I* never employed that moron. Somebody has split us wide open. It isn't just a leak. Somebody was in the Huston Building last night that had no right to be there. This man was supposed to be in Philadelphia. Who *knows* he was in Philadelphia? Check him up, Stein. It's vital."

"I can try to do. But his talk is so foolish I cannot believe he means it. He walks into my room, just now, and asks if I happen to have an old razor blade."

"What for?"

"He says, to scrape his pipe bowl."

Michael Frobisher glared ferociously.

"Ask him to have a drink. Give him plenty. Then talk to him."

"I can try it."

"Go and try it."

Stein stolidly departed on this errand. There were those who could have warned him that it was a useless one.

198

Upstairs, in his room, Morris Craig had taken from his bag ink, pencils, brushes, and all the other implements of a draftsman's craft. He had borrowed a large blotting-pad from the library to do service in lieu of a drawing board.

Stella and Camille had gone out into the garden. The sun was shining.

And over this seemingly peaceful scene there hung a menace, an invisible cloud. The fate of nations was suspended on a hair above their heads. Of all those in Falling Waters that morning, probably Michael Frobisher was the most deeply disturbed. He paced up and down the restricted floor space of his study, black brows drawn together over a deep wrinkle, his eyes haunted.

When Stein came in without knocking, Frobisher jumped around like a stag at bay. He collected himself.

"Well—what now?"

Stein, expressionless, offered a card on a salver. He spoke tonelessly.

"Sir Denis Nayland Smith is here."

chapter 17

"I can tell you, broadly, what happened last night," said Nayland Smith. "It was an attempt to steal the final plans assumed to be locked in Craig's safe."

"I guessed as much," Michael Frobisher replied.

Under drawn brows, he was studying the restless figure pacing to and fro in his study, fouling the air with fumes from a briar pipe which, apparently, Smith had neglected to clean since the day he bought it. Frobisher secretly resented this appropriation of his own parade ground, but recognized that he was powerless to do anything about it.

"The safe was opened."

"You're sure of that?"

"Quite!" Smith rapped, glancing aside at Frobisher. "It was the work of an expert. Dr. Fu Manchu employs none but experts."

"Dr. Fu Manchu! Then it wasn't—"

Smith pulled up right in front of Frobisher, as he sat there behind his desk.

"Well—go on. Whom did *you* suspect?"

Frobisher twisted a half-smoked cigar between his lips.

"Come to think, I don't know."

"But you do know that when a project with such

vast implications nears maturity, big interests become involved. Agents of several governments are watching every move in your dangerous game. And there's another agent who represents no government, but who acts for a powerful and well-organized group."

"Are you talking about Vickers?" Frobisher growled.

"No. Absurd! This isn't a commercial group. It's an organization controlled by Dr. Fu Manchu. In all probability, Dr. Fu Manchu was in Craig's office last night."

"But—"

"The only other possibility is that the attempt was made by a Soviet spy. Have you reason to suspect any member of your staff?"

"I doubt that any Russian has access to the office."

"Why a Russian?" Nayland Smith asked. "Men of influence and good standing in other countries have worked for Communism. It offers glittering prizes. Why not a citizen of the United States?"

Frobisher watched him covertly. "True enough."

"Put me clear on one point. Because a false move, now, might be fatal. You have employed no private investigator?"

"No, sir. Don't trust my affairs to strangers."

"Where are Craig's original plans?"

Michael Frobisher glanced up uneasily.

"In my New York bank."

In this, Michael Frobisher was slightly misinformed. His wife, presenting an order typed on Huston Electric notepaper and apparently signed by her husband, had withdrawn the plans two days before, on her way from an appointment with Professor Hoffmeyer.

"Complete blueprints—where?"

"Right here in the house."

"Were they in the safe that was opened the other night?"

"No, sir—they were not."

"Whoever inspected the plant in the laboratory would be a trained observer. Would it, in your opinion, be possible to reconstruct the equipment after such an examination?"

Michael Frobisher frowned darkly.

"I want you to know that I'm not a physicist," he answered. "I'm not even an engineer. I'm a man of business. But in my opinion, no—it wouldn't. He would have had to dismantle it. Craig and Shaw report it hadn't been touched. Then, without the transmuter, that plant is plain dynamite."

Nayland Smith crossed and stared out at the woods beyond the window.

"I understand that this instrument—whatever it may be—is already under construction. Only certain valves are lacking. Craig will probably complete his work today. Mr. Frobisher"—he turned, and his glance was hard—"your estate is a lonely one."

Frobisher's uneasiness grew. He stood up.

"You think I shouldn't have had Craig out here, with that work?"

"I think," said Smith, "that whilst it would be fairly easy to protect the Huston laboratory, now that we know what we're up against, this house surrounded by sixty acres, largely woodland, is a colt of a different color. By tonight, there will be inflammable material here. Do you realize that if Fu Manchu—or the Kremlin—first sets up a full-scale Craig plant, Fu Manchu—or the Kremlin—will be master of the world?"

"You're sure, dead sure, that they're *both* out to get it?"

Frobisher's voice was more than usually hoarse.

"I have said so. One of the two has a flying start. I want to see your radar alarm system and I want to inspect your armoury. I'm returning to New York. Two inquiries should have given results. One leading to the hideout of Dr. Fu Manchu, the other to the identity of the Soviet agent."

Camille and Stella Frobisher came in from the garden.

"You know," Stella was saying, "I believe we have *discovered* something."

"All we seem to have discovered," Camille replied, "is that there are strange gaps in your memory, and strange gaps in mine. The trouble in your case seems to have begun after you consulted Professor Hoffmeyer about your nerves."

"Yes, dear, it *did*. You see, I had *been* so *worried* about Mike. I thought he was *working* too hard. In his way, dear, he's *rather* a treasure. Dr. Pardoe, who is a *neighbor* of ours, suggested, almost *playfully,* that I consult the professor."

"And your nerves improved?"

"*Enormously.* I began to *sleep* again. But these *queer* lapses came on. I *told* him. He *reassured* me. I'm not at *all* certain, dear, that we have *discovered* anything after all. *Your* lapses began before you had *ever* seen him."

"Yes." Camille was thinking hard. "The trouble

doesn't seem to be with the professor's treatment, after all. Quite apart from which, I have no idea if I ever consulted him at all."

"No, dear—I quite *understand*." Stella squeezed her hand, sympathetically. "You have no *idea* how *completely* I understand."

They were crossing the library, together, when there came a sudden, tremendous storm of barking. It swept in upon the peace of Falling Waters, a hurricane of sound.

"Whatever is it?" Camille whispered.

As if in answer to her question, Sam entered through open french windows. He had removed his topcoat, his cerise scarf, and his slate-grey hat. He wore the sort of checked suit for which otherwise innocent men have been lynched. He grinned happily at Camille.

"Morning, lady."

"Good morning, Sam. I didn't expect to see *you*."

"Pleasant surprise, eh? Same with me." The barking continued; became a tornado. "There's a guy outside says he's brought some dogs."

"*Oh!*" Stella's face lighted up. "*Now* we shall be *safe*! How splendid. Have they sent *all* the dogs?"

"Sounds to me like they sent all they had."

"And a *kennelman*?"

Stella hadn't the slightest idea who Sam was, but she accepted his striking presence without hesitation.

"Sure. He's a busy guy, too."

"I must go and *see* them at once!" She put her arm around Camille. "Do *come* with me, dear!"

Camille smiled at Sam.

"I should love to."

"The guy is down there by the barbed-wire entanglements." Sam stood in the window, pointing. "You can't miss him. He's right beside a truckload of maybe a coupla hundred dogs."

Camille and Stella hurried out, Stella almost dancing with excitement.

Their voices—particularly Stella's—were still audible even above the barrage of barking, when Nayland Smith and Michael Frobisher came into the library.

"You have a fair assortment of sporting guns and an automatic or two," Smith was saying. "But you're low on ammunition."

"Do you expect a siege?"

"Not exactly. But I expect developments."

Nayland Smith crossed to the glazed cabinet and stood before it, pulling at the lobe of his ear. Then he tilted his head sideways, listening.

"Dogs," he rapped. "Why all the dogs?"

Frobisher met his glance almost apologetically.

"It's Mrs. F.'s idea. I do try to keep all this bother from her, but she seems to have got onto it. She ordered a damned pack of these German police dogs from some place. There's a collection of kennels down there like a Kaffir village. She's had men at work for a week fixing barbed wire. Falling Waters is a prison camp!"

"Not a bad idea. I have known dogs to succeed where men and machines failed. But, tell me"—he pointed to the cabinet—"how does this thing work?"

"Well—it's simple enough in principle. *How* it works I don't know. Ground plan of the property. Anyone moving around, when it's connected up, marks his trail on the scoreboard."

"I see."

"I'm having Craig overhaul it, when he has time. If you'll step into my study again for just a minute, I'll get the chart of the layout, which will make the thing more clear."

Nayland Smith glanced at his wrist-watch.

"I can give you just ten minutes, Mr. Frobisher." They returned to Frobisher's study.

Sunshine poured into the empty library. A beautiful Italian casket, silver studded with semi-precious stones, glowed as though lighted by inner fires, or become transparent. The pure lines of the Discus Thrower were sharply emphasized. Barking receded as the pack was removed to the "Kaffir village" erected at Mrs. Frobisher's command.

Then Michael Frobisher came back. Crossing to the desk, he sat down and unlocked a drawer. He took out a chart in a folder, a chart which indicated points of contact surrounding the house as well as free zones. He pressed a bell button and waited, glancing about him.

Stein came in and Frobisher turned.

"Take this to Sir Denis in the study. Tell him I'll be right along in two minutes."

Stein nodded and went out with the folder.

Frobisher dialled a number, and presently:

"Yes—Frobisher," he said nervously. "Sir Denis Nayland Smith is here . . . They're onto us . . . Looks like all that money has been poured down the sewers . . . Huston Electric doesn't have a chance . . ."

He became silent, listening intently to someone on the other end of the line. His eyes kept darting right and left, furtively. Then:

"Got 'em all here, back of the drawer in this desk," he said, evidently in reply to a question . . . "That's none too easy . . . Yes, I'll have it in my hands by tonight, but . . . All right, give me the times."

Frobisher pulled an envelope from a rack and picked up a pencil.

"It mayn't be possible," he said, writing rapidly. "Remember that . . . Nayland Smith is only *one* danger—" He broke off. "Have to hang up. Call you later."

Stein, standing in the arched opening, was urgently pointing in the direction of the study. Frobisher nodded irritably and passed him on his way to rejoin Nayland Smith.

And, as Stein in turn retired, Sam stepped out from behind that Spanish screen which formed so artistic a background for the big walnut desk.

Without waste of time, he opened the drawer which Frobisher had just closed.

Chewing industriously, he studied the scribbled lines. Apparently they conveyed little or nothing to his mind, for he was about to replace the envelope, and no doubt to explore further, when a dull, heavy voice spoke right behind him.

"Put up your hands. I have been watching *you*."

Stein had re-entered quite silently, and now had Sam covered by an automatic!

Sam dropped the envelope, and slowly raised his hands.

"Listen!—happen to have a postage stamp? That's what I was looking for."

Stein's reply was to step closer and run his hands

expertly over Sam's person. Having relieved him of a heavy revolver and a flashlamp, he raised his voice to a hoarse shout:

"Mr. Frobisher! Dr. Craig!"

"Listen. Wait a minute—"

There came the sound of a door thrown open. Michael Frobisher and Nayland Smith ran in. Frobisher's florid coloring changed a half tone.

"What's this, Stein? What goes on?"

"This man searches your desk, Mr. Frobisher. I catch him doing it."

As he spoke, he glanced significantly down at the envelope which Sam had dropped. Nayland Smith saw a look of consternation cross Frobisher's face, as he stooped, snatched it up, and slipped it into his pocket. But there was plenty of thunder in his voice when he spoke.

"I thought so! I thought so right along!"

"Suppose," rapped Smith, "we get the facts."

"The facts are plain! This man"—he pointed a quivering finger at Sam—"was going through my private papers! You took that gun off him?"

"Yes, sir."

"What's he doing armed in my house?" Frobisher roared. "Part of the mystery is solved, anyway—"

A rataplan of footsteps on the stair heralded Morris Craig, in shirt-sleeves, and carrying his reading glasses. He came bounding down.

"Did I hear someone bawling my number?" he pulled up, considered the group, then stared from face to face. "What the devil's all this?"

Michael Frobisher turned now empurpled features in his direction.

"It's what I suspected, Craig. I told you I didn't like the looks of him. There stands the man who broke into the Huston office last night! There stands the man who broke into this house last week. Caught redhanded!"

Sam had dropped his hands, and now, ignoring Stein, he faced his accuser.

"Listen! Wait a minute! I needed a postage stamp. Any harm needing a postage stamp? I just pull a drawer open, just kind of casual, and look in the first thing I see there—"

Craig brushed his forelock back and stared very hard.

"But, I say, Sam—seriously—can you explain this?"

"Sure. I *am* explaining it!"

Nayland Smith had become silent, but now:

"Does the envelope happen to contain stamps, Mr. Frobisher?" he jerked.

"No, sir." Michael Frobisher glared at him. "It doesn't. That inquiry is beside the point. As I understand you represent law and order in this house, I'm sorry—but will you arrange for the arrest of that man."

His accusing finger was directed again at Sam.

"I mean to say," Craig broke in, "I may have missed something. But this certainly seems to me—"

"It's just plain silly," said Sam. "People getting so het up."

Came another rush, of lighter footsteps. Camille and Mrs. Frobisher ran in. They halted, thunderstruck by what they saw.

"*Whatever* is going on?" Stella demanded.

209

"Sam!" Camille whispered — and crossing to his side, laid her hand on his shoulder. "What has happened?"

Sam stopped chewing, and patted the encouraging hand. His upraised spectacles were eloquent.

"Thanks for the inquiry," he said. "I'm in trouble."

"You *are*!" Frobisher assured him. "Sir Denis! This is either a common thief or a foreign spy. In either case, I want him jailed."

Nayland Smith, glancing from Sam to Frobisher, snapped his fingers irritably.

"It is absurd," said Camille in a quiet voice.

"Listen!" Sam patted her hand again and turned to Smith. "I'm sorry. I took chances. The pot's on the boil, and I thought maybe Mr. Frobisher, even right now, might be thinking more about Huston Electric than about bigger things. I guess I was wrong. But I acted for the best."

Michael Frobisher made a choking sound, like that of a faulty radiator.

"You see, Mr. Frobisher," said Nayland Smith, "whatever their faults, your police department is very thorough. James Sampson, an operative of the F.B.I., whom you know as Sam, was placed in the Huston research laboratory by his chief, Raymond Harkness, a long time before I was called in. I regret that this has occurred. But he is working entirely in your interests . . ."

chapter 18

Luncheon at Falling Waters was not an unqualified success. Both in the physical and psychical sense, a shadow overhung the feast.

Promise of the morning had not been fulfilled. Young spring shrank away before returning winter; clouds drew a dull curtain over the happy landscape, blotting out gay skies. And with the arrival of Professor Hoffmeyer, a spiritual chill touched at least two of the company.

Camille experienced a wave of something approaching terror when the stooped figure appeared. His old-fashioned morning coat, his tinted glasses and black gloves, the ebony stick, rang a loud note of alarm within. But the moment he spoke, her terror left her.

"So this," said the professor in his gutteral German-English, "is the little patient who comes to see me not—ha?"

Camille felt helpless. She could think of nothing to say, for she didn't know if she had ever seen him before.

"Never mind. Some other time. I shall send you no

211

account."

Michael Frobisher hated the man on sight. His nerves had remained badly on edge since the incident with Sam. He gave the professor a grip of his powerful fingers calculated to hurt.

"Ach! not so hard! not so hard! These"—Hoffmeyer raised gloved hands—"and these"—touching the dark glasses—"and this"—tapping his ebony stick on the floor—"are proofs that in war men become beasts. I ask you to remember that nails were torn from fingers, and eyes exposed to white heat, in some of those Nazi concentration camps. These things. Mr. Frobisher, could be again . . . While we may, let us be gentle."

Dr. Pardoe treated the professor in a detached way, avoiding technical topics, and rather conveying that he doubted his ability. But not so Mrs. Pardoe. She unbent to the celebrated consultant in a highly gracious manner. A tall, square woman, who always wore black, the sad and sandy Pardoe was not her first love. There had been two former husbands. Nobody knew why. There was something ominous about the angular frame. She resembled a draped gallows . . .

Professor Hoffmeyer addressed much of his conversation to Craig; and Mrs. Pardoe hung on his every word.

"You are that Morris Craig," he said, during luncheon, "who reads a paper on the direction of neutrons, at Oxford, two years ago—ha?"

"The same, Professor. Amazing memory. I am that identical egg in the old shell. Rather stupid paper. Learned better since."

"Modesty is a poor cloak for a man of genius to wear. Discard it, Dr. Craig. It would make me very happy to believe that your work shall be for the good of humanity. This world of ours is spinning—spinning on, to disaster. We are a ship which nears the rocks, with fools at the prow and fanatics at the helm."

"But is there no way to prevent such a disaster?" Mrs. Pardoe asked, in a voice which seemed to come from a condemned cell.

"But most certainly. There could be a committee of men of high intelligence. To serve this committee would be a group of the first scientific brains in the world—such as that of Dr. Craig." For some reason, Camille shuddered at those words. "These would have power to enforce their decisions. If some political maniac threatens to use violence, he will be warned. If he neglects this warning—"

Professor Hoffmeyer helped himself to more fried oysters offered by Stein.

"You believe, then, there'll be another war?" grumbled Frobisher.

"How, otherwise, shall enslavement to Communism be avoided—ha?"

"Unless I misunderstood you," Dr. Pardoe interjected sandily, "your concept of good government approaches very closely to that of an intelligent Communist."

"An intelligent Communist is an impossibility. We have only to separate the rogues from the fools. Yes, Mr. Frobisher, there is danger of another war—from the same quarter as before. Those subhumans of the German General Staff who escaped justice. Those

213

fellows with the traditions of the stockyard and the mentalities of adding machines. Those ghouls in uniform smell blood again. The Kremlin is feeding them meat."

"You mean," Camille asked softly, "that the Soviet Government is employing German ex-officers to prepare another war?"

The secret agent within was stirring. She wondered why this man knew.

"But of course. You are of France, and France has a long memory. Very well. Let France remember. If it shall come, another war, those ignorant buffoons will destroy all, including themselves. This would not matter much if selected communities could be immunized. For almost complete destruction of human life on the planet is now a scientific possibility. It is also desirable. But indiscriminate slaughter—no. The new race must start better equipped than Noah."

When, luncheon over, the professor refused coffee and prepared to take his leave, there was no one present upon whom, in one way or another, he had failed to impress his singular personality. Stella Frobisher flutteringly begged a brief consultation before he left, and was granted one. Mrs. Pardoe made an appointment for the following Friday.

"There is nothing the matter with you," Professor Hoffmeyer told her, "which your husband cannot cure. But come if you so want. You all eat too much. See to it that you permit not here prohibitions, rationings, coupons. Communism knows no boxing laws. Communism strikes at the stomach, first. To this you could never stand up."

A car, in charge of a saturnine chauffeur who had

declined to lunch in the kitchen, declined a drink, and spent his leisure wandering about the property, awaited him. As the professor was driven away, drops of rain began to patter on the terrace.

Night crept unnoticed upon Falling Waters.

Rain descended steadily, and a slight, easterly wind stole, eerie, through the trees. Stella did not merely *ask*, she extended an invitation, to Dr. and Mrs. Pardoe to remain to dinner. But Mrs. Pardoe, already enveloped in a cloak like a velvet pall, reminded her husband that a patient was expected at eight-thirty. Stella saw them off.

"Oh, I'm so *nervous*. It's getting so *dark*. I shan't feel really *safe* until everything is bolted and *barred* . . ."

Coming out of her room, later, having changed to a dinner frock so simple that it must have been made in Paris, Camille almost ran into Sam on the corridor.

"Gee, Miss Navarre! You look like something wonderful!"

"That's very sweet of you, Sam! I had a dreadful shock — yes, truly — when you were discovered today."

"Sure. Shock to me! Ham performance. Must try to make up for it."

"Sam — you don't mind if I still call you Sam?"

"Love it. Sounds better your way."

"Now I know what you are really doing here, I can talk to you — well, sensibly. Dr. Craig thinks, and so, I know, does Sir Denis, that we haven't only to deal with this dreadful Fu Manchu." She paused for a moment after speaking the name. "That there is a

215

Soviet agent watching us, too. Have you any ideas about him?"

Sam nodded. He had given up chewing and abandoned his spectacles. Presumably they had been part of a disguise.

"Working on it right now—and I think we're getting some place."

"Oh! I'm so glad."

"Sure. I got a nose for foreign agents. Smell 'em a mile off."

"Really?"

"Sure." He grinned happily. "You look a hundred per cent Caesar. Excuse my bad spelling!"

He went off along the corridor.

When Camille came down, she found Michael Frobisher busily bolting and barring the French windows.

"Mrs. F.'s got the jumps tonight," he explained. "I have to fix all the catches, myself, to reassure her. Just making the rounds." He gave Camille an admiring smile. "Hope all today's hokum, and the alarm back at the office, hasn't upset you?"

"It's kind of you, Mr. Frobisher, but although, naturally, I am disturbed about it, all the same I am most happy to be here."

"Good girl. Craig has finished his job, and the new diagram and notes are in my safe. That's where they stay. They are the property of Huston Electric, and the property of nobody else!"

As he went out, Morris Craig came downstairs, slim and boyish in his tuxedo. Without a word, he took Camille in his arms.

"Darling! I thought we were never going to be

216

alone again!"

When he released her:

"Are you sure, Morris?" she whispered.

"Sure? Sure of what?"

"Sure that you really meant all you said last night?"

He answered her silently, and at great length.

"Camille! I only wish—"

"Yes?"

"Camille"—he lingered over her name—"I adore you . . . But I wish you weren't going to stay here tonight—"

"What? Whatever do you mean?"

She leaned back from him. Her eyes suddenly seemed to become of a darker shade of blue.

"I mean that, at last, it has dawned on this defective brain of mine that I have done something which may upset the world again—that other people know about it—that almost anything may happen."

"But, Morris—surely nothing can happen *here*?"

"Can't it? Why is old Frobisher in such a panic? Why all the dogs and the burglar alarms? The devil of it is, we don't know our enemies. There might be a Russian spy hiding out there in the shrubbery. There might be a British agent—not that that would bother me—somewhere in this very house."

"Yes," said Camille quietly. "I suppose there might be."

"Above all," Craig went on presently, "there's this really frightful menace—Dr. Fu Manchu. Smith is more scared of him than of all the others rolled into a bundle."

"So am I . . . Listen for a moment, Morris. Sometimes I think I have seen him in a dream. Oh! it sounds ridiculous, and I can't quite explain what I mean. But I have a vague impression of a tall, gaunt figure in a yellow robe, with most wonderful hands, long fingernails, and"—she paused momentarily—"most dreadful eyes. Something, today, brought the impression back to my mind—just as Professor Hoffmeyer came in."

Craig gently stroked her hair. He knew it would be a penal offence to disarrange it.

"Don't get jumpy again, darling. I gather that, in one of your fey moods, you wandered the highways and byways of Manhattan last night instead of keeping your date with the professor. But, certainly, the old lad is a rather alarming personality—although he bears no resemblance to your yellow-robed mandarin. I'm sorry for him, and, of course, his Germanic discourse simply sparkles. But—"

"I didn't mean that the professor reminded me of the man I had dreamed about. It was—something different."

"Whatever it was, forget it." He held her very close; he whispered in her ear: "Camille! The moment we get back to New York, will you marry me?"

But Camille shrank away. The dark eyes looked startled—almost panic-stricken.

"Morris! Morris! No! No!"

He dropped his arms, stared at her. He felt that he had grown pale.

"No? Do you mean it?"

"I mean—oh, Morris, I don't quite know *what* I mean! Perhaps—that you startled me."

"How did I startle you?" he asked on a level, calm note.

218

"You—know so little about me."

"I know enough to know I love you."

"I should be very, very happy for us to go on—as we are. But, marriage—"

"What's wrong with marriage?"

Camille turned aside. A shaded lamp transformed her hair, where it swept down over her neck, to a torrent of molten copper. Craig put his hands hesitantly on her shoulders, and turned her about. He looked steadily into her eyes.

"Camille—you're not trying to tell me, by any chance, that you're married already?"

A door banged upstairs. Stella's voice was heard.

"And *do* make quite sure, Stein—quite *sure*—that there isn't a *window* open." She appeared at the stairhead. "Even with everything *locked*, and the *dogs* loose, I know I shall never *sleep* a wink." She saw Camille below. "Shall *you*, dear?"

"I'm not at all sure that I shall," Camille smiled. "Except that I can see no reason why anything should happen tonight more than any other."

"I must really get *Stein* to *draw* those curtains," Stella declared. "I keep on imagining *eyes* looking in out of the *darkness*. And now, for *goodness'* sake, let's all have a *drink*."

Stein had wheeled in trays of refreshments some time earlier, but had been called away by Mrs. Frobisher in order to bolt a trap leading to a loft over the house.

"May I help?" Camille asked.

And presently they were surrounding the mobile buffet.

Michael Frobisher joined them.

"If you take my advice, my dear," he said to Stella, "you and Miss Navarre will have a good stiff one each after dinner, and turn in early. Think no more about it. Agree with me, Craig?"

Morris Craig stopped looking at Camille long enough to reply:

"Quite. But, if I may say so, somebody should more or less hang about to keep an eye on this thing." He indicated the cabinet above the bookcase. "I have looked over the works and pass same as okay. By the way, Mrs. Frobisher, will the wolf pack be at large tonight?"

"Of course!" Stella assured him. "I have given *explicit* instructions to the *man*. Such a *gentle* character."

"I was wondering," Craig went on, "if the dogs mightn't set the gadget going?"

"Oh, I don't *think* so. They have a *track* of their *own*. *Right* around the *place*—if you *see* what I mean."

"Yes. I have observed the same—from without. Certain hounds of threatening aspect were roaming around within."

"If you remember the layout I showed you," said Frobisher, "showed Nayland Smith, too, there are three gates which would register here"—he crossed and rested a finger on the plan—"if they were opened. Whoever opened one would have Mrs. F.'s dogs on him, I guess. But the dogs can't reach the house."

"Most blessed dispensation," Craig murmured to him. "Although I confess the brutes are rather a comfort, with Dr. Fu Manchu and a set of thugs, plus

220

the Soviet agent assisted by sundry moujiks and other comrades, lined up outside."

Camille was watching Craig in an almost pleading way. Frobisher took his arm, and growled in his ear:

"We'll split up into watches when the women turn in. As you say, somebody ought to be on the lookout right along tonight. Stein can stand watch until twelve. Then I'll take over—"

"No," said Craig firmly, and caught Camille's glance. "I am a party to this disorder, and I'm going to do my bit. After all, I'm accustomed to late hours . . ."

Manhattan danced on, perhaps a slightly more hectic dance, for this was Saturday night, and Saturday night is Broadway night. Rain, although still falling father north, had ceased in the city. But a tent of sepia cloud stretched over New York, so that eternal fires, burning before the altars of those gods whose temples line the Street of a Million Lights, cast their glow up into this sepia canopy and it was cast down again, as if rejected.

Two bored police officers smoked and played crap in Morris Craig's office on top of the Huston Building. And behind the steel door, in an atmosphere vibrant with repressed energy, Martin Shaw worked calmly, and skillfully, to complete the instrument known as a transmuter. The gods of Broadway were false gods. The god enshrined behind the steel door was a god of power.

But the two policemen went on playing crap.

Chinatown was busy, also. Country innocents

gaped at the Chinese façades, the Chinese signs, and felt that they were seeing sights worth coming to Babylon-on-Hudson to see. Town innocents, impressing their girls friends, ate Chinese food in the restaurants and pretended to know as much about it as Walter Winchell knows about everything.

Mai Cha had just ceased to sing in an apartment near the shop of Huan Tsung. Lao Tai had put his last message in the little cupboard.

And upstairs, Huan Tsung reclined against cushions, his eyes closed. The head of Dr. Fu Manchu looked out from the crystal. It might have reminded an Egyptologist of the majestic, embalmed head of Seti, that Pharaoh whose body lies in a Cairo museum.

"To destroy the plant alone is useless, Huan Tsung," came in coldly sibilant words. "I have dealt with this. Otherwise, I should not have risked a personal visit to the laboratory. I sprayed the essential elements with F.SO$_5$. The action is deferred. No—it is necessary also to destroy the inventor—or to transfer him to other employment."

"This may be difficult," murmured Huan Tsung. "Time is the enemy of human perfection, Excellency."

"We shall see. Craig's original drawings were obtained for me by Mrs. Frobisher. Only two blueprints of the transmuter exist. One is in the hands of the chief technician, who is working from it. The other is with a complete set in possession of Michael Frobisher. Drawings of the valves alone remain to be accounted for."

"But Excellency informs me that they, too, are finished."

"They are finished. Give me the latest reports. I will then give you final instructions."

"I shall summarize. Excellency's personal possessions have been removed from the Woolton Building as ordered. They are already shipped. Raymond Harkness has posted federal agents at all points covering Falling Waters — except one; the path through the woods from the highway remains open. Lao Tai will proceed to this point at the time selected. But the dogs—"

"I have provided for the dogs. Continue."

"Provision noted. It is believed but not confirmed that the Kremlin, recognizing the actual plant no longer to be available, hopes to obtain the set of blueprints and the final drawings from Falling Waters before it is too late."

"Upon what does this 'belief' rest?"

"Upon the fact, Excellency, that Sokolov has ordered his car to be ready at ten o'clock tonight — and is taking a bodyguard."

So long a silence followed that Huan Tsung raised his wrinkled lids and looked at the crystal.

The eyes of Dr. Fu Manchu were filmed over, a phenomenon with which Huan Tsung was familiar. The brilliant brain encased in that high, massive skull, was concentrated on a problem. When the film cleared, a decision would have been made. And, as he watched, in a flash the long, narrow eyes became emerald-bright.

"Use the Russian party as a diversion, Huan Tsung. No contact must be made. Koenig has acquainted himself with the zones controlled by the alarm system, and M'goyna is already placed and

223

fully instructed. Mrs. Frobisher has her instructions, also. Use all your resources. This is an emergency. At any moment, now, Nayland Smith will have the evidence he is seeking. Win or lose, I must leave New York before daybreak. Proceed . . ."

chapter 19

Morris Craig sat smoking in a deep leathern arm-chair. The darkened library seemed almost uncannily silent. Rain had ceased. But dimly he could hear water dripping on the terrace outside.

It was at about this moment that the two crap players in his office were jerked violently out of their complacent boredom.

Three muffled crashes in the laboratory brought them swiftly to their feet. There came a loud cry — a cry of terror. Another crash. The steel door burst open, and Martin Shaw, white as a dead man, tottered down the steps!

They ran to him. He collapsed on the sofa, feebly waving them away. A series of rending, tearing sounds was followed by a cloud of nearly vaporous dust which came pouring out of the laboratory in grey waves.

"Stand back!"

"We must close the door!"

One of the men raced up, and managed to close the door. He came down again, suffocating, fighting for breath. A crash louder than any before shook the office.

"What is it?" gasped the choking man. "Is there going to be an explosion? For God's sake"—he clutched his throat—"what's happening?"

"Disintegration," muttered Shaw wildly. "Disintegration. The plant is crumbling to . . . powder."

Pandemonium in the Huston Building. Fruits of long labor falling from the branches. A god of power reduced to a god of clay. But not a sound to disturb the silence of Falling Waters; a silence awesome, a silence in which many mysteries lay hidden. Yet it was at least conducive to thought.

And Morris Craig had many things to think about. He would have more before the night ended.

In the first place, he couldn't understand why Michael Frobisher had been so damnably terse when he had insisted on standing the twelve to four watch. At four, Sam was taking over. Sam had backed him up in this arrangement. Craig had had one or two things to say, privately, to Sam, concerning the deception practiced on him; and would have others to mention to Nayland Smith, when he saw Smith again. But Sam, personally, was a sound enough egg.

So Morris Craig mused, in the silent library.

What was that?

He stood up, and remained standing, motionless, intent.

Dimly he had heard, or thought he had heard, the sound of a hollow cough.

He experienced that impression, common to all or most of us, that an identical incident had happened to him before. But when—where?

There was no repetition of the cough—no sound;

yet a sense of furtive movement. Guiding himself by a sparing use of a flashlamp, he crossed to the foot of the stair. He shone a beam upward.

"Is that you, Camille?" he called softly.

There was no reply. Craig returned to his chair . . .

What was old Frobisher up to, exactly? Why had he so completely lost his balance about the envelope business? Of course, Stein had dramatized it absurdly. Queer fish, Stein. Not a fellow he, personally, could ever take to. Barbarous accent. Clearly, it had forced Nayland Smith's hand. But what had Smith's idea been? Was there someone in the household he didn't trust? . . . Probably Stein.

No doubt the true explanation lay in the fact that Frobisher, having sunk well over half a million dollars in his invention, now saw it slipping through his fingers. It might not be the sort of thing to trust to development by a commercial corporation, but still— rough luck for Frobisher . . .

Then Craig was up again.

This time, that hollow cough seemed to come from the front of the house.

He dropped his cigarette and went over to the arched opening which gave access to Frobisher's study, and, beyond, to the cedarwood dining room. He directed a light along a dark passage. It was empty. He crossed the library again and opened a door on the other side. There was no one there.

Was he imagining things?

This frame of mind was entirely due to the existence of a shadowy horror known as Dr. Fu Manchu. He didn't give a hoot for the Soviet agent, whom- or whatever he might be. Nobody took those fellows seriously. The British agent he discounted entirely. If there had been one, Smith would have known him.

The idea of watching in the dark had been Sam's. As an F.B.I. operative, he had carried the point. Naturally enough, he wanted to get his man. It was a ghostly game, nevertheless. That drip-drip-drip of water outside was getting on Craig's nerves.

Incidentally, where *was* Sam? Unlikely that he had turned in.

But, above all, where was Camille? There had been no chance to make it definite; but he had read the message in her eyes as she went upstairs with Stella Frobisher to mean, "I shall come down again."

Frobisher had retired shortly after the women. "I'm going to sleep — and the hell with it all!"

A faint rustling sound on the stairs — and Craig was up as if on springs.

The ray of his lamp shone on Camille, a dressing gown worn over a night robe that he didn't permit himself to look at. Her bare ankles gleamed like ivory.

"Camille! — darling! At last!"

He trembled as he took her in his arms. She was so softly alluring. He released her and led her to the deep leathern settee, forcing a light note, as he extinguished the lamp.

"Forgive the blackout. Captain's orders."

"I know," she whispered.

He found her hand in his, and kissed her fingers silently. Then, as a mask for his excited emotions:

"I have a bone to pick with you," he said in his most flippant manner. "What did you mean by turning down my offer to make an honest woman of you?

228

Explain this to me, briefly, and in well-chosen words."

Camille crept closer to him in the dark.

"I meant to explain." Her soft voice was unsteady. "I came to explain to you—now."

He longed to put his arms around her. But some queer sense of restraint checked him.

"I'm waiting, darling."

"You may not know—I don't believe you do, even yet—that for a long time, ever so long"—how he loved the Gallic intonations which came when she was deeply moved!—"your work has been watched. At least, you know now, when it is finished, that they will—stick at nothing."

"Who are 'they'? You mean the Kremlin and Dr. Fu Manchu?"

"Yes. These are the only two you have to be afraid of . . . But there is also a—British agent."

"Doubtful about that, myself. How d'you know there's a British agent?"

"Because I am the British agent."

There were some tense moments, during which neither spoke. It might almost have seemed that neither breathed. They sat there, side by side, in darkness, each wondering what the other was thinking. *Drip-drip-drip* went the rainwater . . . Then Craig directed the light of his lamp onto Camille's face. She turned swiftly away, raised her hands:

"Don't! Don't!"

"Camille!" Craig switched the light off . . . "Good God!"

"Don't look at me!" Camille went on. "I don't want you to see me! I had made up my mind to tell you tonight, and I am going to be quite honest about it. I didn't think, and I don't think now, that the work I undertook was wrong. Although, of course, when I started, I had never met *you*."

Craig said nothing . . .

"If I have been disloyal to anyone, it is to Mr. Frobisher. For you must realize, Morris, the dreadful use which could be made of such a thing. You must realize that it might wreck the world. No government could be blind to that."

Subtly, in the darkness, Morris Craig had drawn nearer. Now, suddenly, he had his arm around her shoulders.

"No, Morris! Don't! Don't! Not until I have told you everything." He felt her grow suddenly rigid. "What was that?"

It was the sound of a hollow cough, in the distance.

Craig sprang up.

"I don't know. But I have heard it before. Is it inside the house, or out?"

Switching on the lamp, he ran in turn to each of the doors, and stood listening. But Falling Waters remained still. Then he directed the light onto Camille—and away again, quickly. In a moment he was beside her.

"Morris!"

"Let *me* say something—"

"But, Morris, do you truly understand that I have been reporting your work, step by step, to the best of my ability? Because I never quite understood it. I have been spying on you, all through . . . At last, I couldn't bear it any longer. When Sir Denis came on the scene, I thought I was justified in asking for my release . . ."

Morris's kiss silenced her. She clung to him, trembling. Her heart fluttered like a captive bird released, and at last:

"You see now, Morris, why I felt it was well enough for us to be—lovers. But how could I marry you, when—"

"You were milking my brains?" he whispered in her ear. But it was a gay whisper. "You little redheaded devil! This gives me another bone to pick with Smith. Why didn't he tell me?"

"I was afraid he would! Then I remembered he couldn't . . . Morris! I shall be all bruises! There are traditions in the Secret Service."

At which moment, amid a subdued buzzing sound like that of a fly trapped in a glass, the cabinet over the bookcase came to life!

Camille grasped Craig's hand as he leapt upright, and clung to it obstinately. A rectangle in the library darkness, every detail of the grounds surrounding Falling Waters showed as if touched with phosphorescence.

"We're off!" Craig muttered. "Look!"

A shadow moved slowly across the chart.

"That's the back porch!" Camille whispered. "Someone right outside."

"Don't panic, darling. Wait."

The faint shadow moved on to where a door was marked. It stopped. The buzzing ceased. The chart faded.

"Someone came into the kitchen!"

"Run back and hide on the stair."

"But—"

"Please do as I say, Camille."

Camille released his hand, and he stood, automatic ready, facing that doorway which led to the back premises.

He saw nothing. But he was aware that the door had been opened. Then:

"Don't shoot me, Craig," rapped a familiar voice, "and don't make a sound."

A flashlamp momentarily lighted the library. Nayland Smith stood there watching him—hatless, the fur collar of his old trench coat turned up about his ears. Then Smith's gaze flickered for a second. There came a faint rustling from the direction of the stairs—and silence.

Sam appeared just behind Smith. The lamp was switched off.

"*Smith!*—How did you get in?"

"Not so loud. I have been standing by outside for some time."

"*I* let him in, doc," Sam explained.

"There's some kind of thing slinking around out there," Nayland Smith went on, an odd note in his voice, "which isn't human—"

"What on earth do you mean?"

"Just that. It isn't a baboon, and it isn't a man. Normally, I should form a party and hunt it down. I have a strong suspicion it is some specimen out of Fu Manchu's museum of horrors. But"—Craig, dimly, could hear Smith moving in the dark—"just shine a light onto this."

Craig snapped his lamp up. Nayland Smith stood right beside him, holding out an enlargement of a snapshot. Sam stood at Smith's elbow. Upstairs, a door closed softly.

The picture was that of a stout, bearded man crowned with a mane of white hair; he had small, round, inquisitive eyes.

"Lights out," Smith directed. "I waited at police headquarters for that to arrive. Recognize him?"

"Never saw him in my life."

"Correct. Following his release from a Nazi prison camp, he disappeared. I think I know where he went. But it's of no immediate importance. That is the once celebrated Viennese psychiatrist, Doctor Carl Hoffmeyer!"

"What do you say?"

"Smart, ain't it?" Sam murmured.

"The man New York knew as Professor Hoffmeyer was *Dr. Fu Manchu!*"

"Good God! But he was here today!"

"I know. A great commander must be prepared to take all the risks he imposes on others."

"But he speaks English with a heavy German accent! And—"

"Dr. Fu Manchu speaks every civilized language with perfect facility—with or without an accent! Lacking this evidence, I could do nothing. But I made one big mistake—"

"We all made it," said Sam. "You're no more to blame than the rest."

"Thanks," rapped Smith. "But the blame is mine. I had the Hoffmeyer clinic covered, and I thought he was trapped."

"Well?" Craig asked eagerly.

"He didn't go back there!"

"Listen!" Sam broke in again. "We had three good

233

men on his tail, but he tricked 'em!"

There was something increasingly eerie about this conversation in the dark.

"The clinic remains untouched," Nayland Smith continued. "But Fu Manchu's private quarters, which patients never saw, have been stripped. Police raided hours ago."

"Then where has he gone?"

"I don't know." Nayland Smith's voice had a groan in it. "But all that remains for him to do, in order to complete his work, is here, in this house!"

"Shouldn't we rouse up Frobisher?" Craig asked excitedly.

"No. There are certain things—I don't want Mr. Frobisher to know, yet."

"Such as, for instance?"

"Such as—this is going to hit you where it hurts—that your entire plant in the Huston laboratory was destroyed tonight—"

"What!"

"Quiet, man!" Nayland Smith grasped Craig's arm in the darkness. "I warned you it would hurt. The Fire Department has the job in hand. It isn't their proper province. The thing is just crumbling away, breaking like chocolate. Last report to reach the radio car, that huge telescope affair—I don't know its name—has crashed onto the floor."

"But, Smith! . . ."

"I know. It's bad."

"Thank heaven! My original plans are safe in a New York City bank vault!"

Silence fell again, broken only by a dry cough from Sam, until:

"They are not," Nayland Smith said evenly. "They were taken out two days ago."

"Taken out? By whom?"

"In person, by Mrs. Frobisher. In fact, by Dr. Fu Manchu. Frobisher doesn't know—but the only records of your invention which remain, Craig, are the blueprints hidden somewhere in this house!"

"They were in back of the desk there," Sam mumbled. "But they've vanished."

"You're not suggesting"—Craig heard the note of horrified incredulity in his own voice—"that Mrs. Frobisher—"

"Mrs. Frobisher," said Nayland Smith, "is as innocent in this matter as Miss Navarre. But—we are dealing with Dr. Fu Manchu!"

"Why are we staying in the dark? What happens next?"

"What happens next I don't know. We are staying in the dark because a man called Dimitri Sokolov, a Soviet official in whom Ray Harkness is interested, has a crew of armed thugs down by the lower gate . . . Sokolov seems to be expecting someone."

chapter 20

In the stillness which followed, Morris Craig tried, despairfully, to get used to the idea that the product of months, many weary months, of unremitting labor, had been wiped out . . . How? By whom? He felt stunned. Could it be that Shaw, in a moment of madness, had attempted a test?

"Is poor old Shaw—" he began.

"Shaw is safe," Smith interrupted. "But badly shaken. He has no idea what occurred. Quite unable to account for it—as I am unable to account for what's going on here. I'm not referring to the presence of someone, or some *thing*, stalking just outside the area controlled by the alarms, but to a thing that isn't stalking."

"*What?*" Sam asked.

"The pack of dogs! Listen. Not a sound—but the drip of water. What has become of the dogs?"

"Gee!" Sam muttered. "I keep thinking how dead quiet everything is outside, and kind of wondering why I expect it to be different. Funny I never came to it there was no dogs!"

They all stood motionless for a few moments. That

236

ceaseless drip-drip-drip alone broke the silence of Falling Waters—a haunting signature tune.

"Where is this kennelman quartered?" Nayland Smith asked jerkily.

He was unable to hide the fact that his nerves were strung to concert-violin pitch.

"Middle gate-cottage," came promptly from Sam. "I'll go call him. Name of Kelly. I can get the extension from out here."

"Speak quietly," Smith warned. "Order him to loose the dogs."

Sam's flashlamp operated for a moment. It cast fantastic, moving shadows on the library walls, showing Nayland Smith gaunt, tense; painted Craig's pale face as a mask of tragedy. Then—Sam was gone.

Craig could hear Nayland Smith moving, restless, in darkness. Obscurely Sam's mumbling reached them. He had left the communicating doors open . . . Then, before words which might have relieved the tension came to either, the alarm cabinet glowed into greenish-blue life; muted buzzing began.

"What's this?"

A shadow moved across the plan. It was followed by a second shadow.

"Someone crossing the tennis court!" Craig's voice sounded hushed, unfamiliar. "Running!"

"Someone hot on his heels!"

"Into the rose garden now!"

"Second shadow gaining! First shadow doubling back!"

"That's the path through the apple orchard. Leads to a stile on the lane—"

"But," said Nayland Smith, "if my memory serves

me, the dog track crosses before the stile?"

"Yes. One of the gates in the wire is there."

And, as Craig spoke, came a remote baying.

The dogs were out.

"Listen." Sam had joined them . . . "Say! What's this?"

"Action!" rapped Smith. "Was Kelly awake?"

"Sure. But listen. *Mrs. Frobisher* called him some time tonight, and ordered him to see the dogs *weren't loosed*! Can you beat it? But wait a minute. *Mr.* Frobisher gives him the same order half an hour earlier! . . . Oh, hell! Did you hear that?"

"He's through the gate," said Nayland Smith . . .

The first shadow showed on the chart at a point where a gate in the wire was marked. The second shadow moved swiftly back. A dim blur swept along the track. Baying increased in volume . . . A shot—a second. And then came a frenzied scream, all the more appalling because muted by distance.

"Merciful God!" Craig whispered. "The dogs have got him!"

Nayland Smith already had the french windows open. A sting of damp, cold air pierced the library. There came another, faint scream. Baying merged into a dreadful growling . . .

"Lights!" Smith cried. "Where's the man, Stein?"

As Sam switched the lights up, Stein was revealed standing in the arched opening which led to Michael Frobisher's study. He was fully dressed, and chalky white.

"Here I am, sir."

A sound of faraway shouting became audible. Stella Frobisher ran out onto the stairhead, a robe thrown over her nightdress.

"*Please*—oh *please* tell me what has *happened*? That *ghastly* screaming! And *where* is Mike?"

She had begun to come down, when Camille appeared behind her. Camille had changed and wore a tweed suit.

"Mrs. Frobisher!" Craig looked up. "Isn't the chief in his room?"

"No, he *isn't!*"

Camille's arm was around Stella's shoulders now. "Don't go down, Mrs. Frobisher. Let's go back. I think it would be better if you dressed."

She spoke calmly. Camille had lived through other crises.

"Miss Navarre!" Nayland Smith called sharply.

"Yes, Sir Denis?"

"Go with Mrs. Frobisher to her room, and both of you stay there with the door locked. Understand?"

Camille hesitated for a moment, then: "Yes, Sir Denis," she answered. "Please come along, Mrs. Frobisher."

"But I want to *know* where Mike is—"

Her voice faded away, as Camille very gently steered her back to her room.

Nayland Smith faced Stein.

"Mr. Frobisher is not in his study?"

"No, sir."

"How do you know?"

"I do not retire tonight. I am anxious. Just now, I am in there to look."

"Was the window open?"

Stein's crushed features became blank.

"Was the window open?" Nayland Smith repeated

239

harshly.

"Yes. I closed it."

"Come on, Craig! Sampson—follow!"

"Okay, chief."

Craig and Nayland Smith ran out, Sam behind them.

Stein stood by the opening, and listened. Somewhere out in the misty night, an automatic spat angrily. There was a dim background of barking dogs, shouting men. He turned, in swift decision, and went back through that doorway which led to the kitchen quarters.

He took up the phone there, dialled a number, waited, and then began to speak rapidly—but not in English. He spoke in a language which evidently enlarged his vocabulary. His pallid features twitched as he poured out a torrent of passionate words . . .

Something hard was jammed into the ribs of his stocky body.

"Drop that phone, Feodor Stenovicz. I have a gun in your back and your family history in my pocket. Too late to tip off Sokolov. He's in the bag. Put your hands right behind you. No, not *up*—behind!"

Stein dropped the receiver and put his hands back. There was sweat on his low forehead. Steel cuffs were snapped over his wrists.

"Now that's settled, we can get together."

Stein turned—and looked into the barrel of a heavy-calibre revolver which Sam favored. Sam's grinning face was somewhere behind it, in a red cloud.

"Suppose," Sam suggested, "we step into your room and sample some more of the boss's bourbon?

What you gave me this morning tasted good."

They had gone when Camille came running along the corridor to the stairhead. And there was no one in the library.

"Please stay where you are?" she called back. "I will find out."

A muffled cry came from Stella Frobisher: "Open the *door*! I can't stay *here*!"

Camille raced downstairs, wilfully deaf to a wild beating on wood panels.

"Let me *out*!"

But Camille ran on to the open windows.

"Morris! Morris! Where are you?"

She stood there clutching the wet frame, peering into chilly darkness. Cries reached her—the vicious yap of a revolver—the barking of dogs.

"Morris!"

She ran out onto the terrace. A long way off she could see moving lights.

Camille had already disappeared when Sam entered the library, having locked Stein in the wine cellar. Switching on his flash, he began hurrying in the direction of that distant melee.

The library remained empty for some time. With the exception of Stein, all the servants slept out. So that despairing calls of "Unlock the door, Mike! Mike!" won no response. And presently they ceased.

Then, subdued voices and a shuffling of feet on wet gravel heralded the entrance of an ominous cortege. Upon an extemporized stretcher carried by a half-dressed gardener and Kelly, the grizzled kennel-

241

man, Michael Frobisher was brought in. Sam came first, to hold the windows wide and to allow of its entrance. Nayland Smith followed. There were other men outside, but they remained there.

"Get a doctor," Smith directed. "He's in a bad way."

They lifted Frobisher onto the settee. He still wore his dinner clothes, but they were torn to tatters. His face and his hands were bloody, his complexion was greyish-purple. He groaned and opened his eyes when they laid him down. But he seemed to be no more than semi-conscious, and almost immediately relapsed.

Kelly went out again, with the empty stretcher. A murmur of voices met him.

"I know Dr. Pardoe's number," said the gardener, a youthful veteran whose frightened blond hair had never lain down since the Normandy landing. "Shall I call him?"

His voice quavered.

"Yes," rapped Smith. "Tell him it's urgent."

As the man hurried away to the phone in the back premises:

"Nothing on him?" Sam asked.

"Not a thing! Yet he was alone—with the dogs, God help him! I believe he was running for his life. Perhaps from that monstrosity I had a glimpse of when I first arrived."

"That's when he lost the plans!" said Sam excitedly. "He must have broken away from—whatever it was, and tried to cross the track. Lord knows what was after him, but I guess he was crazy with fright. Anyway, he figured the dogs were locked up—"

"When, in fact, they were right on top of him!

Failing Kelly's arrival, I could have done nothing. Rouse somebody up. Get hot water, lint, iodine. Rush."

As Sam ran to obey, Raymond Harkness stepped in through the open window. He wore a blue rainproof, a striped muffler, and a brown hat. He was peeling off a pair of light suede gloves. He looked like an accountant who had called to advise winding up the company.

"It's not clear to me, Sir Denis, just what happened out there tonight—I mean what happened to Frobisher."

"You can see what happened to him!" said Smith drily.

"Yes—but how? Sokolov was waiting to meet him, but he never got there—"

"Somebody else met him first!"

"Sokolov's thugs made the mistake of opening fire on our party." Harkness put his gloves in his pockets. "Otherwise, I'm not sure we should have had anything on Sokolov—"

The wounded man groaned, momentarily opened his eyes, clenched his injured hands. He had heard the sound of someone beating on a door, heard Stella's moaning cry:

"Let me out! Mike!"

"Don't," Frobisher whispered . . . "allow her . . . to see me."

As if galvanized, Nayland Smith turned, exchanged a glance with Harkness, and went racing upstairs.

"Mrs. Frobisher!" he called. "Mrs. Frobisher— where are you?"

"I'm *here*!" came pitifully.

Smith found the locked door. The key was in the lock! He turned it, and threw the door open.

Stella Frobisher, on the verge of nervous collapse, crouched on a chair, just inside.

"Mrs. Frobisher! What does this mean?"

"She — Camille — *locked* me in! Oh, for *heaven's* sake, *tell* me: *What* has happened?"

"Hang on to yourself, Mrs. Frobisher. It's bad, but might be worse. Please stay where you are for a few minutes longer. Then I am going to ask you to lend us a hand. Will you promise? It's for the good of everybody."

"Oh, *must* I? If *you* say so, I suppose — "

"Just for another five minutes."

Smith ran out again, and down to the library. His face was drawn, haggard. In the battle to save Frobisher from the dogs, with the added distraction of a fracas between F.B.I. men and Sokolov's bodyguard at the lower gate, he had lost sight of Craig! Camille he had never seen, had never suspected that she would leave Mrs. Frobisher's room. Standing at the foot of the stair:

"Harkness," he said. "Send out a general alert. Dr. Fu Manchu not only has the plans. He has Camille Navarre and the inventory, also . . ."

The police car raced towards New York, casting a sword of light far ahead. Against its white glare, the driver and a man beside him, his outline distorted by the radio headpiece, were silhouettes which reminded Nayland Smith of figures of two Egyptian effigies. The glass partition cut them off completely from those in the rear. It was a special control car, normally sacred to the deputy commissioner . . .

"We know, now," said Harkness, "where the attack came from."

"We know many things when it's too late," Nayland Smith answered. "I knew, when I got back tonight, that Michael Frobisher was an agent of the Soviet, knew the Kremlin had backed those experiments. I knew Sokolov was waiting for him . . ."

His crisp voice trailed off into silence.

Visibility in the rear was poor. So dense had the fog become, created by Smith's pipe, that Harkness experienced a certain difficulty in breathing. Motorcycle patrolmen passed and repassed, examining occupants of all vehicles on the road.

"That broken-down truck wasn't reported earlier," Harkness went on, "because it stood so far away from any gate to Falling Waters. What's more, it hadn't been there long."

"But the path through the woods has been there since Indian times," Smith rapped. "And the truck was drawn up right at the point where it reaches a highway. How did your team come to overlook such an approach?"

"I don't know," Harkness admitted. "It seems Frobisher didn't think it likely to be used, either. It doesn't figure in the alarm plan."

"But it figured in Fu Manchu's plan! We don't know—and we're never likely to know—the strength of the party operating from that truck. But those who actually approached the house stuck closely to neutral zones! His visit today—a piece of dazzling audacity—wasn't wasted."

Traffic was sparse at that hour. Points far ahead had been notified. Even now, hope was not lost that the truck might be intercepted. Both men were thinking about this. Nayland Smith first put doubt into words.

"A side road, Harkness," he said suddenly. "Another car waiting. Huan Tsung is the doctor's chief of staff—or used to be, formerly. He's a first-class tactician. One of the finest soldiers of the old regime."

"I wish we could pin something on him."

"I doubt if you ever will. He has courage and cunning second only to those of his distinguished chief."

"There's that impudent young liar who sits in the shop, too. And I have reports of a pretty girl of similar type who's been seen around there."

"Probably Huan Tsung's children."

"His *children*!" Even the gently spoken Harkness was surprised into vehemence. "But—how old is he?"

"Nearing eighty-five, I should judge. But the fecundity of a Chinese aristocrat is proverbial . . . Hullo! what's this?"

The radio operator had buzzed to come through.

"Yes?" said Harkness.

"Headquarters, sir. I think it may be important."

"What is it?" Nayland Smith asked rapidly.

"Well, sir, it comes from a point on the East River. A young officer from a ship tied up there seems to have been saying good night to a girl, by some deserted building. They heard tapping from inside a metal pipe on the wall, right where they stood. He spotted it was *Morse*—"

"Yes, yes—the message?"

"The message—it's just reached headquarters—says: '*J. J. Regan here. Call police. . . .*' There's a party setting out right now—"

"Regan? *Regan?* Recall them!" snapped Smith. "Quickly!"

Startled, the man gave the order, and then looked back. "Well, sir?"

"The place to be covered, but by men who know their job. Anyone who comes out to be kept in view. Anyone going in to be allowed to do so. No suspicion must be aroused."

The second order was given.

"Anything more?"

"No." Nayland Smith was staring right ahead along the beam of light. "I am trying to imagine, Harkness, how many times the poor devil may have tapped out that message. . . "

chapter 21

Camille's impressions of the sortie from the house were brief, but terrifying.

That tragedy, swift, mysterious, had swept down on Falling Waters, she had known even before she ran from her room to prevent Stella Frobisher going downstairs. The arrival of Nayland Smith had struck a note of urgency absent before. Up to this moment, she had counted her confession to Morris the supreme ordeal which she must brave that night.

But, when she returned upstairs (and she knew Sir Denis had seen her), apprehension grew. She had dressed quickly. She realized that something was going to happen. Just what, she didn't know.

Then she heard someone running across the rose garden which her window overlooked. She laid down the cigarette she was smoking, went and looked out. She saw nothing. But it was a dark night. She wondered if it would be wise to report the occurrence. But before decision was reached had come that awful cry—shots—the baying of dogs.

Stella Frobisher, evidently wide awake, had come out of her room. Camille had heard her hurrying along the corridor, had run out after her . . .

It had been difficult, inducing Stella to return. Camille had succeeded, at last.

But to remain locked in, whilst Morris was exposed to some mysterious but very real peril—this was a trial to which Camille was unable to submit. It was alien to all her instincts.

She felt mean for locking Stella into her own apartment, but common sense told her that Mrs. Frobisher could be only a nuisance in an emergency.

Then had come that stumbling rush in cold, clammy darkness towards the spot where, instinctively, she knew Morris to be—in danger. Whilst still a long way off, she had seen that horrifying mix-up of dogs and men. Morris was there.

Almost unconsciously she had cried his name, "Morris! Morris!"

By means of what miracle Morris heard her voice above the tumult Camille would never know—unless her heart told her; for a second disturbance had broken out not far away: shots, shouting.

But he did.

He turned. Camille saw someone else, probably the kennelman, joining in the melee. Perhaps she was outlined against lights from the house; but Morris saw her, began to run towards her. He seemed to be shouting. His behavior was wild.

Something—it felt like a damp, evil-smelling towel—was dropped suddenly over her head . . .

And now?

Now she lay on a heap of coarse canvas piled up in

a corner of what seemed to be a large, and was unmistakably a dilapidated, warehouse: difficult to assess its extent for the reason that the only light was that of a storm-lamp which stood on the roughly paved floor close to where Camille lay.

Another piece of this evidently abundant sacking had been draped over one side of the lantern, so that no light at all reached a great part of the place. There was a smell of dampness and decay with an overtone which might have been tea. It was very still, except that at the moment when she became conscious of her surroundings, Camille thought she had heard the deep, warning note of a steamer's whistle.

The impression was correct. The *S. S. Campus Rex* had just pulled out from a neighboring berth, bound for the River Plate. Her third officer was wishing he knew the result of his message to the police and wishing he could have spent one more night with his girl friend . . .

A scuffling sound brought Camille to her feet at a bound.

There were rats around her in the darkness!

She had physical courage such as, perhaps, few women possess. But the presence of rats had always set her heart beating faster. They terrified her.

Swaying slightly, she became aware of a nausea not due merely to fright. There was an unpleasant taste on her palate. A sickly sweet odor lingered, too, in her disordered hair. Of course, she might have expected it. The towel, or whatever had been thrown over her head, must have been saturated with an anaesthetic.

She stood quite still for a moment, trying to

conquer her weakness. The scuffling sound had ceased. In fact, she could detect no sound whatever, so that it might have been some extra sense which prompted her to turn swiftly.

Half in the light from the storm-lamp and half in shadow, a tall man stood watching her.

Camille stifled a cry almost uttered, and was silent.

The man who stood there wore a long, loose coat with a deep astrakhan collar. A round cap, of Russian type, and of the same close black fur, was on his head. His arms were folded, but the fingers of his left hand remained visible. They were yellow, slender fingers, prolonged by pointed fingernails meticulously manicured.

His features, lean, ascetic, and unmistakably Chinese, were wholly dominated by his eyes. In the lantern light they gleamed like green jade.

"Your sense of hearing is acute," he said, his harsh voice subdued. "I thought I moved quite noiselessly."

And, as he spoke, Camille knew that this was the man who had haunted her dreams.

"Who are you?" She spoke huskily. "What am I doing here?"

"You asked me a similar question not long ago. But you have forgotten."

"I have never seen you in my life before—as you are now. But I *know* you! You are Dr. Fu Manchu!"

"Your data are inaccurate. But your inference is correct. What are you doing here, you say? You are suffering the inconvenience of one who interferes with my plans. I regret the crude measures used by Koenig to prevent this interference. But his promptitude saved the situation."

"Where is Dr. Craig?" Camille demanded breathlessly. "What have you done to him?"

He watched her through narrowed eyes and unfolded his clasped arms before he replied:

"I am glad your first, your only, concern is for Dr. Craig."

"Why?"

"Presently, you shall know."

And something in that expression, "You shall know," brought sudden revelation to Camille.

"You are the man who called himself Professor Hoffmeyer!"

"I congratulate you. I had imagined my German-English to be above reproach. I begin to wonder if you cannot be of use to me. As Professor Hoffmeyer, I have been observing the life of Manhattan. I have seen that Manhattan is Babylon reborn—that Manhattan, failing a spiritual revolution, must fall as Babylon fell."

"Where is Dr. Craig?" Camille repeated, mechanically, desperately. "Why have I been brought *here*?"

"Because there was no other place to which they could bring you. It surprises me, I confess, that a woman of such keen perceptions failed to learn the fact that Michael Frobisher was a Communist."

"A Communist? Mr. Frobisher? Oh, no—he is a Socialist—"

"Socialism is Communism's timid sister. Michael Frobisher is an active agent of the Soviet Union. Before his marriage, he spent many years in Moscow. Dr. Craig's invention was financed by the Kremlin. Had Frobisher secured it for them, he was promised a post which would have made him virtual dictator of

252

the United States."

Even in her desolation, despair, this astounding fact penetrated to Camille's mind.

"Then he was clever," she murmured.

"Communism *is* clever. It is indeed clever to force the world's workers to toil and sweat in order that their masters may live in oriental luxury."

"Why do you tell me all this? Why do you talk to me, torture me, but never answer my question?"

"Because, even now, at this eleventh hour, I hope to convert you. You heard me, as Professor Hoffmeyer (the professor, himself, is at work in one of our research centers), outline a design for world harmony. To the perfecting of this design I have given the labor of a long life."

He paused. A soft, weird cry came from somewhere near. Its effect upon Camille was to shatter her returning composure. To her it portended a threat of death. Had Nayland Smith heard it, he would have recognized the peculiar call of a dacoit, one of that fraternity of Burmese brigands over whom Dr. Fu Manchu exercised a control hitherto unexplained.

"What was it?"

Camille breathed, rather than spoke, the words.

"A warning. Do not allow it to disturb you. My plans are complete. But my time is limited. You are anxious concerning Dr. Craig. I, too, am anxious. For this reason alone I have talked to you so long. I hope you can induce him to accept the truth. You may succeed where I have failed."

He turned and walked away. Camille heard the creak of an opening door.

The warning which Camille had construed as a message of evil omen had been prompted by something occurring on the nearby river front.

To any place, the wide world over, where men go down to the sea in ships, night brings no repose. So that, even at this hour, Manhattan danced on. Winches squealed. Anchor chains rattled. Sea boots clattered along decks. Lights moved hither and thither. Hoarse orders were shouted. Tugboats churned the muddy river. And the outgoing tide sang its eternal song of the ocean, from which it had come, to which it returned.

But no one had time to pay attention to a drunken sailor who came reeling along past deserted dock buildings, blacked-out warehouses, stumbling often, rebuking himself in an alcoholic monotone. He steadied up every once in a while against a friendly doorway, a lamp standard, or a stout pipe.

Once such pipe seemed to give him particular satisfaction. Perhaps because it ran down the wall of a building marked for demolition upon the doors of which might still be read the words: "Shen Yan Tea Company."

This pipe he positively embraced, and, embracing it, sank ungracefully to the sidewalk, and apparently fell asleep.

A few minutes later he had established contact with Regan. He, too, was a Morse expert.

"Yes. John Regan here. Huston Electric. Who are you?"

"Brandt. Police officer. Where are you?"

"Old strong room. Basement. Don't know what

building."

"Shout. I may hear you."

"Dumb."

This message shook Brandt.

"How come?"

"Injection. Attacked in lab Friday night. Get me out."

"Starving?"

"No. But food and water finished."

"Any movement overhead right now?"

"Yes. Someone up there."

"Hang on. Help coming."

The drunken sailor woke up suddenly. He began to strike matches and to try to light a cigarette. He remained seated beside the pipe. These matches attracted the attention of a patrolman (who had been waiting for this signal) and who now appeared from somewhere, and approached, swinging his club.

But the matches had also attracted the attention of another, highly skilled observer. So that, as the police officer hauled the drunk to his feet and led him off, the call of a dacoit was heard in the empty warehouse.

"This was formerly the office of a firm of importers known as the Shen Yan Tea Company," said Dr. Fu Manchu. "An old friend of mine had an interest in that business."

Morris Craig swallowed—with difficulty. He had by no means recovered from the strangling grip of those unseen fingers. He would have liked to massage his bruised throat. But his wrists were secured by

255

metal clamps to the arms of his chair, a remarkable piece of furniture, evidently of great age; it had a curious, domed canopy which at some time might have been gilded. He was helpless, mad with anxiety about Camille, but undaunted.

"Strange coincidence," he replied huskily. "No doubt this attractive and comfortable rest-chair has quite a history, too?"

"A long one, Dr. Craig. I came across it in Seville. It dates from the days of the Spanish Inquisition, when it was known as the Chair of Conversion. I regret that of all those treasured possessions formerly in the Woolton Building, this one must be left behind."

"Seems a great pity. Cozy little piece."

Fu Manchu stood watching him, his long narrow eyes nearly closed, his expression indecipherable. There was that about the tall, fur-capped figure which radiated power. Craig's nonchalance in the presence of this formidable and wholly unpredictable man demanded an immense nervous effort.

"It may be no more than a national trait, Dr. Craig, but your imperturbable façade reminds me of Sir Denis."

"You flatter me."

"You may not know, but it will interest you to learn, that your capture, some hours ago, was largely an accident."

"Clearly not my lucky day."

"I doubt if the opportunity would have arisen but for the unforeseen appearance of Miss Navarre. In running to join her, you ran, almost literally, into the arms of two of my servants who were concerned only in retiring undetected."

"Practically left the poor fellows no choice?"

"Therefore they brought you along with them."

"Friendly thought."

Dr. Fu Manchu turned slowly and crossed the office. Like the adjoining warehouse, it was lighted only by a partly draped lantern which stood on a box beside the Spanish chair. The floor, in which were many yawning gaps, was littered with rubbish. A boarded-up window probably overlooked a passage, for there was no sound to suggest that a thoroughfare lay beyond.

Directly facing Craig, a long, high desk was built against the cracked and blackened wall. In this wall were two other windows, level with the top of the desk, and closed by sliding shutters. And on the desk Craig saw a metal-bound teak chest.

Very deliberately Dr. Fu Manchu lifted this chest, came back, and set it on the box beside the lantern. His nearness produced a tingling nervous tension, as if a hidden cobra had reared its threatening hood.

"Amongst those curious possessions to which I referred," he continued in his cold, conversational manner (he was unlocking the chest), "Is the mummied head of Queen Taia, known to the Egyptians as the 'witch queen.' Her skull possesses uncommon characteristics. And certain experiments I am carrying out with it would interest you."

"Not a doubt of it. My mother gave me a mummy's head to play with when I was only four."

"The crystal sets we use in our system of private communication also accompany me to headquarters. This"—he opened the chest—"which I borrowed from there, must never leave my personal possession until I return it."

Morris Craig's hands — for only his wrists were constrained — became slowly clenched. Here, he felt, came the final test; this might well be the end.

What he expected to happen, what he expected to see, he could not have put into words. What he did see was an exquisitely fashioned model of just such an equipment as that which had been destroyed in the Huston Building!

The top, front, and sides of the chest were hinged, so that the miniature plant, mounted on its polished teak-base, lay fully open to inspection. Wonder reduced Morris Craig to an awed silence. Apart from the fact that there were certain differences (differences which had instantly flamed his scientific curiosity), to have constructed this model must have called for the labor of months, perhaps of years.

"I don't understand." His voice sounded unfamiliar to him. "I don't understand at all!"

"Only because," came in cold, incisive tones, "you remain obsessed with the idea that you *invented* this method of harnessing primeval energy. The model before you was made by a Buddhist monk, in Burma. I had been to inspect it at the time that I first encountered Sir Denis Nayland Smith. Detailed formulae for its employment are in my possession. You, again, after a lapse of years, have solved this problem. My congratulations. Such men were meant to reshape the world — not to destroy it."

Dr. Fu Manchu began to reclose the chest.

"I don't understand," Craig repeated. "If the principle was known to you, as well as the method of applying it — and I can't dispute that it was —"

"Why did I permit you to complete your experiments? The explanation is simple. I wanted to know if you *could* complete them. On my arrival, the main plant had already been set up in the Huston laboratory. I was anxious to learn if the final problem would baffle you. It did not. Such a man is a man to watch."

Dr. Fu Manchu locked the teak chest.

"Then it was *you* who destroyed my work?"

"I had no choice, Dr. Craig. Your work was destined for the use of the Kremlin. I have also your original plans, and every formula. The only blueprints existing I secured tonight. One danger, only, remains."

"What's that?"

"Yourself."

And the word was spoken in a voice which made it a sentence of death.

Dr. Fu Manchu carried the chest across the littered room, and opened what looked like a deep cupboard. He placed the chest inside, and turned again to Craig.

"You will have noted that I am dressed for travel, Dr. Craig. My time is limited. Otherwise, I should employ less mediaeval methods to incline your mind to reason. You seem to have failed to recognize me as Professor Hoffmeyer, but a committee such as I spoke of when we met already exists. It is called the Council of Seven. In our service we have some of the best brains of every continent. We have wealth. We are not criminals. We are idealists —"

A second of those wailing cries, the first of which had terrified Camille, checked his words. Craig started.

"I may delay no longer. You have it in your power, while you live, to destroy all our plans. Therefore, Dr. Craig—I speak with sincere regret—either you must consent to place your undoubted genius at my disposal—or you must die."

"The choice is made."

"I trust not, yet."

Dr. Fu Manchu opened one of the sliding shutters over a long desk. It disclosed an iron grille through which crept a glimmer of light.

"Miss Navarre!" There was no slightest change of tone, of inflection in his strange voice. "You were anxious about Dr. Craig. Here he is—perfectly well, as you may judge for yourself."

And Morris Craig saw Camille's pale face, her eyes wide with terror, hair disordered, staring at him through the bars!

A torrent of words, frenzied, scathing, useless words, flooded his brain. But he choked them back—rejected them; and when he spoke, in a whisper, he said simply:

"Camille!"

"When we move"—Nayland Smith's expression was very grim—"we must be sure the net has no holes in it. We have Regan's evidence that there are people in that building. We know who put Regan there. So we know what to expect. Is our cordon wide enough?"

"Hard to make it wider," Harkness assured him. "But these old places are honeycombs. There are sixty men on the job. I have sent for the keys of all the adjoining buildings."

"We daren't wait!" Smith said savagely. "Fu Man-chu has destroyed the last possibility of Craig's invention being used—except *Craig* . . . we daren't wait."

"Report coming through," said Harkness.

The report was one which might have meant next to nothing. A cry had been heard, more than once, in the neighborhood of the closely covered building, which at first hearing had been mistaken for the cry of a cat. Repeated, however, doubt had arisen on this point.

"That settles the matter!" rapped Smith. "It was the call of one of his Burmese bodyguard! Fu Manchu is there."

"There was a pleasant simplicity," Dr. Fu Manchu was saying, "in the character of the unknown designer of this chair. I fear I must start its elementary mechanism. The device bears some resemblance to a type of orange-squeezer used in this country."

He stood behind Craig for a moment; and Craig became aware of a regular, ticking sound, of vibrations in the framework of the chair: he clenched his teeth.

"I am going to ask Miss Navarre to add her powers of persuasion to mine. If you prefer to live—in her company—to devote yourself to the most worthy task of all, the salvation of men from slavery or from destruction, I welcome you—gladly. You are a man of honor. Your word is enough. It is a bond neither you nor I could ever break. Do you accept these terms?"

"Suppose I don't?"

Morris Craig had grown desperately white.

"I should lock the control, which, you may have noted, lies under your right hand: an embossed gold crown. I should prefer to leave it free. You have only to depress it, and the descent will be arrested. Choose—quickly."

"Whichever you please. The result will be the same."

"Words worthy of Molotov! The time for evasion is past. I offer you life—a life of usefulness. I await your promise that, if you accept, you will press the control. Your doing so will mean, on the word of an English gentleman, that you agree to join the Council of Seven. Quickly. Speak!"

"I give you my word"—Morris Craig's eyes were closed; he spoke all but tonelessly—"that if I press the control it will mean that I accept your offer."

Dr. Fu Manchu crossed to the door behind which he had placed the teak chest. As he passed the grilled window:

"The issue, Miss Navarre," he said, "rests with *you*."

He went out, closing the door.

"No! No! Come back!" Camille clutched the iron bars, shook them frantically. "Come back! . . . No! *No!* Merciful God! stop him! Morris! Agree! Agree to anything! I—I—can't bear it . . "

The domed canopy, its gilding barely touched by upcast lantern light, was descending slowly.

"Don't look at me. I shall—weaken—if you look at me . . ."

"Weaken! Morris, darling, listen to me! Dr. Fu Manchu is a *madman*! There can be no obligation to

262

a madman . . . I tell you he's mad! Press the control! Do it! *Do* it!"

The canopy continued to descend, moving in tiny jerks which corresponded to audible ticks of some hidden clockwork mechanism. It was evidently controlled by counterweights, for Craig found the chair to be immovably heavy.

He closed his eyes. He couldn't endure the sight of Camille's chalk-white, frenzied face staring at him through those bars. A parade of heretics who had rejected conversion passed before him in the darkness, attired in the silk and velvet, the rags and tatters, of Old Seville. Their heads lolled on their shoulders. Their skulls were crushed. . . .

"Morris! Have you no pity for *me*? Is this your love . . ."

He must *think*. "A bond neither you nor I could ever break." Those had been the words. That had been the bargain. If he chose life, Dr. Fu Manchu would claim his services.

"Camille, my dearest, you have faced worse things than this—"

"I tell you he is mad!"

"Unfortunately, I think he's particularly sane. I even think, in a way, he has the right idea."

Tick-tick . . . Tick-tick . . Tick-tick. In fractions of an inch, the canopy crept lower.

"I shall lose my reason! O God in heaven, hear me!"

Camille dropped to her knees, hands clasped in passionate supplication. Kneeling, she could no longer see Morris. But, soon, she must look again.

Meaningless incidents from the past, childish memories, trivial things; submerged dreams of a future that was never to be; Morris's closed eyes; the open, dreadful eyes of Dr. Fu Manchu: all these images moved, in a mocking dance, through her prayers . . .

A whistle skirled—a long way off. It was answered by another, nearer.

Camille sprang up, clutched the bars.

The canopy almost touched Morris's head. His eyes remained closed.

She began to scream wildly:

"*Help! Help!* Be quick! Oh, be quick!" She clenched her hands so tightly that her nails bit into the palms, and spoke again, a low, quivering whisper: "Morris! He may be right, as you think. Morris! for my sake, believe it. There is—just time."

Craig's hand twitched, where it rested over the gilded crown of life which meant . . . He did not open his eyes.

There came a wild tide of rushing footsteps, a charivari of shouting, crash of axes on woodwork . . .

"This way! This—way!"

Camille's attempted cry was only a strangled murmur. She supported herself by clinging with all but nerveless fingers to the grille.

"A light in here!" came a breathless shout.

The blade of an axe split through woodwork covering the only exterior window in the office. A second blow—a third. The planking was wrenched away. Outside lay a stone-paved passage crowded with men.

"Good God! Look! Here's Dr. Craig, sir!"

"Be quick!" Camille murmured, and fought to check insane laughter which bubbled to her lips.

"Under his hand . . . that knob . . . *press* it. . . "

Nayland Smith, his dark complexion oddly blanched, forced his way through. The canopy just touched the top of Craig's head. A wave of strength, sanity, the last, swept over Camille.

"Sir Denis! That — gold crown — on the arm of the chair . . . Press it."

Nayland Smith glanced swiftly towards the grille, then sprang to the chair, groped for and found a crown-shaped knob under Craig's listless fingers, and pressed it, pressed it madly.

The clockwork sound ceased. He dropped to one knee.

"Craig! Craig!"

Beads of sweat trickled from a limp forelock down an ivory face, but there was no reply.

Morris Craig had fainted.

"This is the way she pointed, but maybe it didn't mean anything." Sam had joined the party. "Gee! Those two must have gone through hell!"

"Fortunately," said Nayland Smith, "they have youth on their side. But the ordeal was — ghastly. It is characteristic of Fu Manchu's unusual sense of humor that the canopy is made so that it cannot descend any further. Craig was in no danger! Hullo! what's this?"

They had reached the foot of a short flight of stone steps, the entrance to which Craig had mistaken for a deep cupboard. Harkness was in front, with two men. Two more followed. All carried flashlamps.

An empty passage, concrete-floored, extended to

left and to right.

"Take a party left, Harkness. I'll take the right."

Ten paces brought Smith to a metal door in the wall. He pulled up. Retreating footsteps, the sound of which echoed hollowly, as in a vault, indicated that the other party had found nothing of interest so far.

"Job for a safebreaker," Sam grumbled. "If this is the way he went, he'll get a long start."

"Quiet!" rapped Nayland Smith. "Listen."

He beat a syncopated tattoo on the metal with his knuckles. Harkness's party had apparently turned in somewhere. Their footsteps were no more than faintly audible.

Answering knocks came from the other side of the door!

"Regan!" Sam exclaimed.

Smith nodded. "This is what he called the strong room. Quiet again."

He rapped a message—listened to the reply; then turned.

"This scent is stale," he said shortly. "Regan states nobody has passed this way tonight."

"We must get Mr. Regan out, right now." Sam spoke urgently. "You, back there, O'Leary, report upstairs there's an iron door to be softened. Poor devil! Guess he's dumb for life!"

"Not at all," Nayland Smith assured him. "The effect wears off after a few days—so I was recently informed by my old friend, Dr. Fu Manchu."

He spoke bitterly—a note of defeat in the crisp voice. What had he accomplished? He could not even claim credit for saving the blueprints from Soviet hands. Some servant of Fu Manchu's had secured them before the dogs attacked Frobisher—

"Sir Denis!" came a distant, excited hail. "This way! I think we have him!"

Nayland Smith led the run back to where Harkness and two men stood before another closed door near the end of a passage which formed an L with that from which they had started.

"I think it's an old furnace room. And I saw a light in there!"

"Don't waste time! Down with it!"

Two of the party carried axes. And they went to work with a will. The door was double-bolted on the inside, but it collapsed under their united onslaughts. A cavity yawned in which the rays of Nayland Smith's lamp picked out an old-fashioned, soot-begrimed boiler, half buried in mounds of coal ash.

"Be careful!" he warned. "We are dealing with no ordinary criminal. Stand by for anything."

They entered cautiously.

The place proved to have unexpected ramifications. It was merely part of what had been an extensive cellarage system. They groped in its darkness, shedding light into every conceivable spot where a fugitive might lie. But they found nothing. A sense of futility crept down upon all, when a cry came:

"Another door here! I heard someone moving behind it!"

Over the debris and coal dust of years, they ran to join the man who had shouted. He stood in what had evidently been a coal bunker, before a narrow, grimy door.

"It's locked."

Keen axes and willing hands soon cleared the

obstacle.

A long, sloping passage lay beyond. Up its slope, as the door crashed open, swept a current of cold, damp air. And, halfway down, a retreating figure showed, a grotesque silhouette against reflected light from his dancing flashlamp.

It was the figure of a tall man, wearing a long coat and what looked like a close-fitting cap.

"By God!" Smith shouted, "Dr. Fu Manchu! This leads to the river—"

He broke off.

Sam had hurled himself into the passage, firing the moment he crossed the threshold of the shattered door! The crash of his heavy revolver created an echo like a thunderstorm. Nayland Smith, following hard behind, saw the figure stumble, pause—run on.

"Cease fire there!" he shouted angrily.

But Sam's blood was up. He either failed to hear the order, or wilfully ignored it. He fired again— then, rapidly, a third time.

The tall figure stopped suddenly, dropped the flashlamp, and crumpled to the damp floor.

"You fool!" Nayland Smith's words came as a groan. "This was no end for the greatest brain in the world!"

He forced his way past Sam, stopped, and turned the fur-capped head. As he did so, the fallen man writhed, coughed, and was still.

Nayland Smith looked into a face scarcely human, scarred, a parody of humanity—a face he had never seen before—the face of M'goyna . . .

He stood up very slowly. The dark, sloping passage behind him seemed to be embossed with staring eyes.

"Outmanoeuvred!" he said. "Fu Manchu played for time. This poor devil was the last of his rearguards. He has slipped through our fingers!"

chapter 22

Ten days later, Nayland Smith gave a small dinner party at his hotel to celebrate the engagement of Camille Mirabeau (Navarre) to Dr. Morris Craig. When the other guests had left, these three went to Smith's suite, and having settled down:

"Of course," said Smith, in reply to a question from Camille, "the newspapers are never permitted to print really important news! It might frighten somebody."

"Quite a lot has leaked out, though," Craig amended. "The cops gave it away. Poor old Regan has been pestered since I resigned. But although he can chatter quite acidly again, he won't chatter to reporters."

"How's Frobisher?"

"Rotten. He'll recover all right, but carry a crop of scars."

"Does his wife know the truth?"

"Couldn't say. What do you think, Camille?"

Camille, lovely in her new-found happiness and a Paris frock, shrugged white shoulders.

"Stella Frobisher is like a cork," she said. "I think

she can stay afloat in the heaviest weather. But I don't know her well enough to tell you if she suspects the truth."

"The most astounding thing which the newspapers haven't reported," Nayland Smith remarked after an interval, "concerns the body of that ape man — almost certainly the creature of which I had a glimpse at Falling Waters. He's been examined by all the big doctors. And they are unanimous on one point."

"What is that?" Camille asked.

"They say the revolver bullets didn't kill him."

"What?" Craig exclaimed.

"They state, positively, that he had been dead *many years* before the shooting!"

And Camille (such was the strange power of Dr. Fu Manchu) simply shook her red head and murmured. "But that is impossible."

Yes — that was impossible. It was also impossible, no doubt, that Dr. Fu Manchu had visited New York, and perhaps, as a result of his visit, given a few more years of uneasy peace to a world coquetting with war. And so, Manhattan danced on . . .

"Our two Russian acquaintances" — Nayland Smith rapped out the words venomously — "have been quietly deported. But what I really wanted to show you was this."

From the pocket of his dinner jacket he took a long, narrow envelope. It had come by air mail and was stamped "Cairo." It was addressed to him at his New York hotel. He passed it to Camille.

"Read it together. There was an enclosure."

And so, Craig bending over Camille's shoulder, his cheek against her glowing hair, they read the letter, handwritten in copperplate script:

Sir Denis—

It was a serious disappointment to be compelled to leave New York without seeing you again. I regret, too, that M'goyna, one of my finer products, had to be sacrificed to my safety. But a little time was necessary to enable me to reach the boat which awaited me. I left by another exit. I greet Dr. Craig. He is a genius and a brave man. But his keen sense of honor is my loss. Will you, on my behalf, advise him to devote his great talents to non-destructive purposes? His future experiments will be watched with interest. I enclose a wedding present for his bride.

There was no signature.

Camille and Morris Craig raised their eyes, together.

On his extended palm Nayland Smith was holding out a large emerald. And as Camille, uttering a long, wondering sigh, took the gem between her fingers, Nayland Smith reached for his dilapidated pouch and began, reflectively, to load his blackened briar.